THE
END OF THE
WORLD

THE
END OF THE
WORLD

MATT MCGRATH

To order additional copies of this book, contact:
Xlibris
AU TFN: 1 800 844 927 (Toll Free inside Australia)
AU Local: (02) 8310 8187 (+61 2 8310 8187 from outside Australia)
www.Xlibris.com.au
Orders@Xlibris.com.au
856796

He danced solemnly, the feathers on his ankles scratching in the dirt and sending up clouds of dust. Ululating tones issued from his throat and lulled the senses of the onlookers. The gold on his wrists flashed in the firelight and became dull and coppery again. He sang about the feathered snake and the way the rain came and went.

The feathered snake rode on the clouds and blew a fierce wind from its mouth. Lightning flashed and thunder rolled. "eyo Quetzalcoatl" intoned the priest. "Ha" sang the crowd. The dancer rolled his head from side to side and shrugged his shoulders as if in a coughing fit. He opened his mouth and drank in the rain. The fire, which was lit under a rocky outcropping sputtered and hissed. Flutes shrilled and percussive instruments were struck and the chanting of the throng became frenzied. The crowd clapped and stamped and pressed closer around the dancer. He seemed possessed and his eyes were unfocused and half closed.

The priest took some thorns and chewed on them until blood ran down from his mouth. He shrieked and called out to the feathered snake and then fell down in a trance upon the ground.

He lay still for a few heartbeats and then began to writhe and slither on the ground. He built strange mounds in the dust and knotted the tassels on his cloak. He seemed to slowly become aware of his surroundings and he threw his arms out wide in a bold gesture and spoke to the populous "Quetzalcoatl has spoken to me of rain and wind and he brings tidings of ill fortune to our people."

"When the sun has sunk three times below the horizon, there will be a tremor of the earth and our houses and crops will be swallowed. The darkness will descend and there will be no light. The sun itself is sick and threatens to fall from heaven." The people wailed and shook with terror, the priest bowed his head and uttered a keening sound.

"What can we do to assuage his anger? What sacrifice is demanded?" asked a man from the crowd.

The priest shook and convulsed. He made a choking sound and said "sacrifice is always demanded. The nature of the sacrifice is not to be divined."

Gradually, the crowd dispersed. The priest scampered behind the rock and Treoc was left alone at the gathering place. He picked up a discarded feather from the priest's costume and examined it carefully. The quills on one side of the feather were brushed down and on the other side they pointed upwards giving it a dishevelled, animated appearance. The quills moved in his hand trembling slightly and sending a prickling sensation through his fingers. He tried to drop the feather but it remained glued to his hand sending shockwaves through his hand. He shook his hand and the feather fell to the ground. He stuck his throbbing, bruised fingers under his arm and groaned.

He stuck his fingers in his mouth, bit on his thumb and drew blood. His vision swam and he fell to the ground. All was dark He heard a rushing sound like the beating of leathery wings and he felt the breath of the feathered snake. "Three more days" it seemed to say. "Three more days and all is mine. I will send dark clouds and black rain, the earth will open and swallow standing stones and the stars will change their dance and traverse by a different path. I will supp on warm blood and gnaw the sinewy limbs of my devotees and they will know their true purpose."

Shaken and weak the boy awoke from his reverie. He knew he should tell someone about the vision, which had left him scared and confused. He resolved to tell his father about the vision and to see if he could obtain some healing herbs from his grandmother.

He tried to get his father's attention but the man was preoccupied with feathering arrows. He made the flights skilfully and with great attention to detail and he had no time for his son's stories. His grandmother was more receptive and she made a poultice from basil and rosemary and bound his hand with a paste made from llama milk. The old woman stroked his cheek and made much of him. She told him of the rain and thunder gods and how they played skittles in the heavens. He smiled when she told him of Xlalxi's vanity and Tluci An's trickery.

Finally, when the boy appeared to have forgotten why he came his grandmother asked him. "Child what happened in the clearing? What evil thing did you grasp to have such a burn?"

His grandmother had not been with the people at the clearing and had not heard the priest's pronouncement. "Ah the end of the world!" she exclaimed. "I have often wondered what kept the gods from destroying this place. Clearly everything is far from perfect."

"For every end of the world that we have had some lucky mortal has survived to found a new tribe in the next world. That, young one is your task. Think about the old songs that we teach you. Watch how the knots bunch up on the prince's ropes and pay attention to the pattern of the rain drops and the things you can sniff in your morning milk."

"When I picked up the feather I could not let it go and my hand began to shake. It caused me great pain and I was afraid." said the boy.

"The priest is drowning in the serpent's venom and everything he touches is infected with Quetzalcoatl's burning spittle. Do not go near the shaman! He will perish before the world's end I prophesy and those that raise a hand against him will also die in great pain."

"He speaks the truth then?"

"He knows a truth and that is what he preaches. The world will end for many and soon. I am sure it will end for me. I can meet the gods instead of die in my bed like a sick old crone. You are charged to live young thing....Think about the old heroes and the caves underground. Think about the roads of fire and ice and the caverns where the sun never shines. Men hide from the gods but the old embrace them. Sing songs is all I can do apart from cook and bind a child's hand. To be in the old songs is a rare privilege. I do not want to go unceremoniously into the dark. Let the thunder roll and Tlaloc's lightning flash!"

The boy left his grandmother. His hand no longer felt sore but he was troubled by his grandmother's words. He went to see his father, hoping that the man had finished with the arrows and that he would eventually speak to him.

The boy's father tended the arrows carefully. He took the feathers in his hand, combed the bristles outward to make a flight and fixed the feather to the arrow shaft. Then he repeated the process, again and again with rapt, solemn attention.

He eventually noticed his child. "Help me." He said in an inviting tone. The boy took up an arrow shaft and cautiously took hold of a condor feather. He fitted the feather to the shaft and placed the arrow on the pile with the others. His father hummed softly to himself and began to chant. "oye ye e oh" – a long meaningless series of sounds that he sang to meditate. He continued for what seemed like an age until he caught the boy looking at him expectantly.

"What is wrong boy?", his father asked.

"The priest says the world will end. I hurt my hand on his feather. Will the world end?"

"Sometime undoubtedly" replied the man. "I have my work to do, my arrows to make and I do not know what else to do. We must simply live and wait to die or should the gods will it to escape in some fashion not yet foreseen."

"You are young and have not seen as much death as I. All living things die and our time on earth is brief. You are my heir and the prized child of our family I will be gone, you may live on or perhaps perish with me, though the thought naturally pains me. The priests predict these things and they come to pass. They predict war and famine and we fight and starve. They see evil omens in the stars and we are struck by plague. Such is the way of the world. I think though that the gods sometimes favour our kind. Think about the old stories. How the serpent god led our forefathers through a subterranean cavern to safety when fire destroyed the world."

"Tell me this story father, I want to hear something hopeful."

"The sun was angry with the people and the creatures of the earth. He shone burning red and low in the sky and his rays blinded the people when they looked up. The mountains erupted and lava flowed through the land. Choking black smoke killed many in their beds and the others fled to the rivers and waters and the caves in the earth. The waters gave people succour at first and they thanked the rain god. They drank and immersed themselves in the cooling element and sang songs to the rain god and the master of the distant ocean. Their relief was short lived however, the molten rock and slag flowed into the river, poisoning it and making it too hot to bear. The people in the caves became trapped by falling rocks and the population dwindled. The animals suffered too and even the jaguar grew lean.

The brothers Hlali and Xluxu were in a cavern with a spring. They drank the cool waters of the spring and stared at the strange rocks in the cavern. The rocks looked like the rain god and the feathered snake, they resembled a small man with a large head and a reclining king with his tongue stuck out. The boys waited in the dimly lit cavern not knowing what to do. There was no food to be had. They bowed their heads and tried to sleep. As they closed their eyes they heard a slithering sound. A snake slithered over Hlali's shoulder and onto the floor, it crossed the cave and disappeared into a small opening in the far wall. The boys, seeing this as a sign from the feathered snake, decided to investigate the opening. The crack in the far wall of the cave was small as it was blocked by rubble and fallen stones. The brothers dug and scraped against the far wall and eventually the shifted enough of the stones to discover an opening to another cavern. They crawled through the opening into a large cavern with a gently descending floor. There was almost no light and they hesitated to go any further. They thought about the world outside and considered turning back.

Outside, the fire rained down from the mountains. Ash filled the sky and the air was foul and poisonous, nearly everyone was dead and the vegetation burned. Then the heavy ashen clouds opened and the rain fell but the fire did not abate. The rain god forsook mankind as well and joined the sun in his purge of the earth. The rain hissed in the hot waters and sizzled on the blackened stones.

The few remaining people wept in terror and awaited their destruction. There was little food to be had. The forest burned and the animals were in hiding or dead. The fish floated, bloated and poisoned and the people were afraid to eat them and the crops were long covered in ashes or burnt. The wind alone remained as a potential source of relief. A healing breeze from the sea was hoped for but the wind god ignored the people and the ash and the rain were relentless.

The boys heard the rain in the cavern and thought about turning back but as they went to leave the serpent blocked their path and raised to strike at them. They fled into the darkness and ran down the dark tunnel into the black unknown.

They came to a running river the water swirled and roared over sharp black stones. The brothers moaned in pain as they crossed the river, cutting their feet on the stones. They came to the far bank of the river and lay exhausted in the grey sand.

They rested by the river bank, dim light came from far above and through a distant chasm they could view the clouds and the swirling smoke that seemed to be swept away from the opening by a strange force, a contrary wind or some poorly understood air current from the cave. They saw shapes in the water, fish shot through the dark water and snapped at the air. The boys tried to catch them in their fingers and caught fists full of gritty sand and splashed in the unforgiving water.

Eventually, Xluxu caught a fish and they shared the raw flesh greedily in the dim light of the cavern. They slept by the river and awoke hours later to total darkness. The air smelt sweeter and they were somehow encouraged. Xluxu felt that the sun god slept and the rain and fire deities had given up or gone elsewhere to wage their perpetual wars.

They followed the stream as it broadened and quickened and they came to a waterfall and an enormous chasm. The black water roared over the broken stones into the darkness below and white foam licked the boulders and slicked over the cupped ponds into unknown depths. The boys heard voices and came across three humans. An old man and two women, whom they did not know. The man said they came from afar, near the sea and that they had fled pestilence and destruction, following the water and climbing a long way until they came to where they were now. The man said they had seen Tlaloc's face after a lightning bolt hit the hills around them. The rain god was full of wrath and we fled but he did not block our path. We climbed and followed the water and came to this place.

We were chased here by a snake, an animal sacred to Quetzalcoatl. I think the wind god wanted us to live and spared us for some inscrutable reason. We doubt not at all that our tribesmen are all dead and our people are no more.

"I fear that for us the same is true" said the man. "We are the only ones left."

"Then we should stay here and wait for a sign" said Hlali.

They stayed by the river and waited. Nothing happened for a long time and they caught fish when they could and ate them raw with the relish of the starving. Eventually, the sky above the river grew clear and they saw the stars. They were heartened that the clouds had departed and that the heavens had not been completely destroyed. They waited longer until driven at last by hunger they attempted to climb down the waterfall into the vast cavern beyond. They made the climb with difficulty and came to the base of the waterfall. Here the water was deep and there were no fish to be found. They were loath to go further out of fear of Tlaloc and the things the old man and his daughters had seen. They lingered at the base of the waterfall until they saw a snake slither from under a rock and disappear into the blackness. They heard a hiss and followed the sound the snake was in a corner, forked tongue out and it slithered left and right in a frustrated pattern as if mesmerised or somehow furious. No one dared approach too closely and the old man hummed a tune the boys did not know. The snake slowed in its dance and its forked tongue darted in and out and licked the black rocks. They saw a natural staircase, wonderous and unlooked for and encouraged by this seeming miracle they began to ascend. They climbed the staircase and came to an opening. Here was a vale in the hills that the gods had spared! It was marvellous, with blue water and green grass. A condor could be seen in the sky above and the air was sweet and unpolluted.

They came to a land known to our people and are our ancestors. This is the story of how a few survived the end of the world but this is not the only time the world was destroyed. It is said that the sun has chosen to destroy the earth four times and some of the other times the destruction was so complete that an entirely new race of people came into being. We do not know much about the previous destructions of the world or the strange gods that ruled in these long-gone times. There is war and destruction in heaven as well as on the earth and the gods themselves are not secure on their thrones. If the end of the world comes again it might be complete or some of us might be saved like the boys or the old man and his daughters. There is no way for us to know what is in store. The heavens are an unstable place and the gods are fickle. I have little doubt that the powers desire retribution and man has little time upon the earth. However, we cannot stop living and await destruction. There are arrows to make and crops to harvest and much work even for a young boy with a sore hand."

The boy had become mesmerised by the story. He had heard it before from his grandmother and from an old story teller in the village but this was the first time his father had ever told him the story and it was the longest and most elaborate version of the tale that he had heard. He did not know about the previous ages of the world and the destruction that the sun wrought upon the earth. Everyone knew that sun was vengeful and a jealous ruler of the earth but to question the sun's ways was not his place and some things were taboo and not to be spoken of, even with one's father or closest kin.

"The priest will speak to us of the world's end again. Of that I am sure." said the man. The boy nodded and went to see his grandmother to find out if she had any errands for him to run.

The priest was in a state of high irritation. The graven images of the gods accused him. The open hollow mouth of Tlaloc roared at him and the feathered snake's image seemed to spit venom. The populace exasperated him. Time for ameliorating the needs of the gods was short and the people appeared to be numb to their certain fate.

The stars spoke of destruction, so did the wind, so did the entrails that he had read. Sacrifice was clearly required. The gods he thought, did not ask for it, the time for placating them was long gone and they danced and shook with the anticipation of war and havoc.

He would have to speak to the people again. They were subdued and miserable but they seemed to have little energy. No one had tried to do anything that day, even to run away. They did not doubt him, he thought but they were too stupid to take any sort of action and they feared the gods and did not understand them.

He had hopes that they could be placated with blood. He had slaughtered animals: birds and a guinea pig today and had smeared the blood on stones near the statues. The priest thought about all he knew about Tlaloc and the other gods that dealt in retribution and death.

He hoped that tonight, when the moon went black they would come to their senses and think about the approaching end of the world with more than resignation and hopelessness.

The gods demanded sustenance – therein lay the people's hope for survival. Sacrifice, obeisance, penitent behaviour, all were required merely to draw the attention of the divine. Avoiding divine wrath was almost impossible. Everything spoke of this, the plague, the failed crops, the warring tribes that attacked from the jungles to the east. All of these factors indicated a supernatural malevolence that threatened the lives and welfare of the Inca people.

The priest had endured self-inflicted pain merely to gain the attention of the lesser gods. He thought that this had led to his faint and his vision. He shuddered to think about what might be required to placate the wrathful major gods. Burnings, killings, the destruction of graven images, wailing and dancing. All were not to be excluded from the potential list of methods for contacting the deities.

The priest struck a rock to his left with his fist and shrieked then he bowed his head and hummed a throaty tune. He was the son of a priest and had lived his whole life in the company of the shocking, unforgiving supernatural world.

He breathed heady drugs and incenses, cut himself in ritual ceremonies and sacrificed all manner of animals, birds and insects to the diverse supernatural beings that held sway in the Inca pantheon.

The priest could remember a time when he had had a normal name, Tluci, he had been called as a boy but ever since he was as tall as a man's shoulders he had been known as Xlacalaccu - he who makes offerings. As a young child he had run about the village and spent time idly or diligently interacting with its denizens. He knew how lazy the people could be, how they would find some piece of busy work around a warm fire to do to stop from having to go out into the cold, how the farmers cursed the rain god and the women the gods of increase, and, knowing him for a priest's son occasionally ventured a thrown stone or a stealthy kick.

He could have complained to his father but this would have meant disturbing the man's meditation- something that would most certainly be met with punishment. He received long and arduous instruction in the ways of the gods and how they must be served and he was educated in the arts of knot tying, mathematics and astronomy.

He would talk to the people again soon. The message was too important for him to wait much longer. He would demand that they provide some sacrifice for the gods. He knew that many of them would sacrifice something in their homes but this was not enough. Public ritual was clearly required and he wanted to know how seriously the people took him. He was convinced that a cataclysmic event was about to occur. Astronomical events like these occurred seldom and boded ill for everyone. His visions spoke of destruction and perdition for all of the people and he held out little hope for anything. He knew however that they were obliged to act or to face retribution even more terrible than might otherwise be the case.

He beat upon a golden gong on a shelf in the temple and called to his acolytes. The other priests came running to meet him and were full of concern about the approaching end of the world.

"I too have read of it in the entrails of an eagle" said one of the priests.

"The stars are certain" said another.

"There is no doubt that the gods are angry" said a third.

The chief priest called for coca leaves and sweet-smelling spices to be brought to the temple. He would imbibe what he could and see what he could see. There was little time for augury and he knew he would have to mobilise the priests and the population in some act of penance this very day.

"We have little time. The gods cry vengeance and they must be appeased. Sacrifice is required and a show of open penitence."

The coca leaves and the incense were brought to the priest by a servant and the priest hastily took hold of them and tossed the vegetation onto a burning brazier. The brazier flared with greenish light for a few moments before a pungent grey-white smoke began to fill the air and the priest threw his head back, flared his nostrils and breathed the fumes greedily in.

His voice became hoarse and his movement jerky and tense. "Quetzalcoatl brings a fresh wind from the north." He said. "He wants to see his people and has news for us. We shall all assemble by the lake before the rising of the sun. I am to bring a silver sickle and a silver bowl to catch blood. These items must be found immediately!" The priest collapsed with a flourish on the floor and his acolytes made haste to seek out the sickle and the bowl.

The temple was enormous with many rooms and hidden nooks for all sorts of treasures. The acolytes made haste to search for the precious items and no stone was left unturned. The silver bowl was found almost straight away but no one could find a silver sickle. The daggers that they had were unsuitable. None of them were curved like the moon as was required.

Thinking that the ritual weapon had been taken elsewhere, perhaps to a far-flung altar or sacred grove in another part of the valley, the priests sent messengers to every grotto and dell that was dedicated to a deity.

There were many sacred places around the village, in the forest and in the foothills of the mountains. Every available runner and servant boy was underway, searching for the silver sickle. They asked the old priests that watched the moon or the mountain springs if they had seen the holy blade but no one had seen such a dagger. The moon rose higher in the night sky and its sickly green-white glow bathed the earth in phosphorescent light.

A messenger reached the foot of the tallest mountain, the eldest as it was called and met a wild eyed man with a forked beard. "Tonight, the moon will be swallowed whole and the ships that sail in the sky will come loose from their courses" predicted the madman. "The heavens are not immutable and the gods will tilt the balance until all things fall and fail. We have little time left and our destruction is certain. There is no hope in Quetzalcoatl except perhaps to hope for a quick death before the true destruction comes." He told the messenger to be gone. He said he should go and spend his last hours on the earth with his family and to pay no heed to the priests for there was no way to circumvent the coming destruction. The heavens were in chaos and soon the moon itself would be extinguished. All the omens point to this event. "The sun and the moon chase each other around the heavens and the sun will soon be devoured by the moon, which will itself perish in the attempt to swallow the sun. Run and hide from the destruction!"

The servant was determined to find the knife, however, he had no wish to displease the priests and hoped for some divine protection in view of the dire omens that the holy men read. He asked the wild man about a silver sickle.

The man seemed dazed and then spoke absently. "Such a sickle have I indeed for use in a sacred rite. I cut the wings from a bat and smeared the animal's blood on a sacred stone. Tlaloc spoke to me and made clear our doom. You cannot take the knife but I will give it to one of the priests should they come. Although I doubt that they will come if they can read the heavens as well as a humble shaman like me. There is no hope left."

Fearing delay the messenger turned on his heel and hurried as fast as he could back to the temple to fetch a priest that might pry the knife away from the madman. The high priest himself came to hear of the commotion and resolved to set out for the shrine immediately. The messenger and the high priest came to the shrine after and arduous hour of climbing. The high priest was fatigued but the urgency remained in him. He wanted the sickle at all costs. The madman was nowhere to be seen but they could see the shrine - a black rough-hewn rock covered with dried blood. The high priest went to the altar and there wrapped in animal skins was the sickle. The high priest tested the edge on his thumb. The blade was indeed sharp and the keen edge would find a use before sunrise.

The high priest made an obeisance to the black god of rain and woe, Tlaloc. The gods were angry and confused, already warring in heaven and ill-disposed to look with favour on any offering from earth. The high priest pricked his thumb and let a drop of blood roll onto the altar. Then he wrapped the knife in its skins and stowed it in a satchel.

As they turned to leave, the man with a forked beard blocked the path. "Holiest of us all, please leave me my knife. I will sacrifice a beast again before sunrise. I was away on the hunt for something suitable. There is no hope to be had. I want only deeper knowledge so that I can die with my eyes open facing the destruction. There is still much confusion but destruction is certain."

"We are never certain of the gods' will until it comes to pass" replied the high priest. "I read destruction in the natural world and I have foreseen it. I will do my best to appease the gods. Make way for we are in haste."

"Let me keep the knife revered one. It has strange powers. Other hands do not suit it, it belongs to me and I am the instrument of the gods when I use it. It is their will that I retain it and worship here until the end comes." The man with the forked beard remained rooted on the spot.

The high priest flew into a rage. He drew the knife, rushed forward and slit the wild man's throat from ear to ear. The messenger trembled with terror and the priest snorted and bellowed like an enraged animal. "Quetzalcoatl waits! We must go with all possible haste to the shores of the lake. Run ahead and fetch the silver bowl from the temple."

The messenger flew past the priest and hurried for all he was worth down the steep path, stumbling and sliding all the way. The shaken messenger reached the village in ten short minutes and told the startled villagers "Blood has been shed. The priest shed the blood of a holy man. What terrible things Quetzalcoatl demands I do not know but what has come to pass is bad enough. Go to the lakeside in the hour before dawn, all of the auguries say that we must prostrate ourselves before the gods or perish but have a care as it may be the last thing you do."

The people were concerned and asked "What did the holy man do that his blood was shed and what do the soothsayers say? Can we do anything to avert the world's end?"

The messenger shook his head and dashed on to the temple to seek the silver bowl. In the temple the priests were making great commotion all was being made ready for a religious procession to the lakeside. Feathers were bound to arms, golden circlets placed around necks and ankles, girdles of furs and strange feathers gathered in the deeps of the forest were girt round the waists of the acolytes and soothsayers, red and yellow dyes were applied liberally and the priests reeked of incense, bitter herbs and an unrecognisable oil. The silver bowl lay on a bed of leaves. Four men stood about it making ready to bear it reverently in the procession."

The messenger explained the urgency with which the bowl was required and the priests reluctantly agreed to let him bear it to the high priest. "Sacrifices have already been made" muttered the messenger, "More are required. I shudder at the thought of what Quetzalcoatl might demand to avert our destruction."

The high priest felt powerless. No divine messenger came to him, the blood he had spilt gave him no power, no mystic elevation of the senses or drug-like catatonic trance ensued. The gods ignored him he was sure and danced their dance of death in the uncertain heavens. He needed the sickle, he knew he needed it for the ceremony at the lakeside. He needed to fill the bowl with steaming blood and pour it into the sea. Of that much he was clear and he needed to do this often. He had thought to offer the blood of a dedicated animal. Shedding human blood for sacrifice was unusual he did not know if the gods would accept this and he feared his people. They would turn on him should disaster strike too soon or too late. If his prophecy was misread by a day their faith would be shaken and they would destroy him out of fear.

He was certain of the stars. The moon would block out the sun and the earth would be in darkness, then there was to be an eruption, the mountain would not remain silent and with that eruption would come their certain doom. Old legends spoke of hope for a few. In past cataclysms, people had escaped by hiding deep in the earth. He feared the gods would elect to totally destroy mankind. This had happened before and new peoples were created out of the stone by the gods.

Perhaps this was no cycle of destruction and rebirth but the ultimate death of the sun. The gods themselves were not immortal and although they lived a much longer span than man they too ultimately perished. The people spoke of the end of the world but few had a real inkling of what this meant.

They feared the future but did not understand what it meant. That the end was perilously close. The high priest knew that much would come to an end should the best they could hope for come to pass and total destruction be averted. Should he fail in his duty to sacrifice, then the heavens would wreak total destruction on them all and no one would be spared. Their civilisation would come to an end as would humanity itself and the very birds and trees would suffer perhaps beyond recovery.

He had visions of steaming blood in a bright silver vat. He poured the blood on the water and it boiled with appreciation. He felt the snake's breath and the exhilarating closeness of the godhead, the feathered snake would come to him. Quetzalcoatl had some use for humanity still. Although the god was tricksy and bargained hard with his supplicants.

The path was rough and the high priest had a long way to go. It was further to the shores of the lake than it was to the temple and he had to look around carefully and check his bearings to be certain of the way. The mountain shrine was a place he could not remember visiting before. He was sure he must actually have visited it at some stage in the past. As high priest he was initiated in all the rituals that the gods demanded and he had worshipped at virtually every altar and grotto. Still he could not remember going to the mountain grotto before and the man with the forked beard was a stranger – unknown to him by name or reputation. He wondered if the man had really been alive or If he was a demon conjured up by the gods to tempt him into rash and possibly blasphemous action. Such messengers were not unknown, there was the corn wrestler and the red parrot and other apparitions that were sent by the gods. Perhaps to slay such a one was not a bad omen. Quetzalcoatl had set him a test and he felt certain that he had passed. The visions of blood were intoxicating, they were the way to appease the snake god. In his mind's eye he saw the god's forked tongue flicker in and out.

He passed some shrubs and a rocky outcrop and heard the footfalls of a llama. The beast emerged from behind the rocks. It was not shy and he held still, wondering if this was another omen or simply a natural event. The animal looked at him sidelong, chewed and whistled to itself and then turned and galloped back up the path. Superstitiously, the priest followed the animal. The beast had not crossed his path by chance and was certain to lead him somewhere important. The llama led him to a black rock. The beast galloped around the black rock and seemed agitated by it. The high priest recognised an object sacred to Tlaloc. Tlaloc's colour was black and the stone was squat and rectangular like the god himself. Tlaloc willed destruction. That was humanity's standing view of his interaction with the earth. It was something Tlaloc hated and wished to destroy. People made sacrifices to Tlaloc out of fear but no one could make a pact or bargain with this god so bent as he was on the annihilation of the human race.

The high priest hesitated to approach the rock more closely. He could see dried blood on top of the stone and he thought he could pick out worn carvings on the underside. Was he doing Tlaloc's will and leading man closer to destruction? Sacrificing the llama here might be the start of the end knowing the god's dark sense of humour. Tlaloc cannot be appeased. Failure to do some homage might also be fatal and the priest was struck by indecision. The time was passing quickly and soon he would have to make his way to the side of the lake. Tlaloc had made him disturbed. He went to the stone and ran his fingers along the carvings underneath. They were extraordinarily sharp and he cut his hand.

The carvings resembled saw shaped teeth and the lips of a hateful mouth and the high priest thought he heard a deep booming voice saying "Soon all will perish and the dark lands will be mine." The llama had bolted and he was alone with the stone and the knife in a dark grotto. He put his hand under his arm and tried to leave the grotto but he tripped over a tree root on the ground and fell. He heard the booming voice laughing and noticed that the sickle had fallen out of his hand and clattered against the stone. He picked up the blade and examined it and found to his annoyance that it was notched.

Would Quetzalcoatl accept the sacrifice with the notched blade? Would the baleful influence of Tlaloc be felt during the ceremony at the lakeside? The high priest did not know. Limping now he made his way back down the path and continued along the road in the direction of the river.

The messenger was making haste along the path with the bowl. He did not encounter the priest and made his way to the appointed place at the side of the lake. This was a place where treasures had been cast into the river for centuries to please the gods. A golden glimmer could be seen in the waters during the day and it was taboo to swim in the water.

The messenger sat cross-legged on the sand by the water and waited for the arrival of the others: the high priest, the procession and the crowd from town that would accompany the procession.

The people in the town were restless. Their imminent doom became apparent to them with the religious preparation occurring at the temple and the dire predictions of the priests. They knew they had little time left on this earth and their hearts were heavy. They ate greedily, without sparing meat or corn for the next day as they knew that their time was short.

Treoc and his family joined the procession keeping to the rear well away from the painted priests. They looked menacing and were under the influence of strange potions and noxious fumes. Treoc's father and grandmother were fearful now, their earlier stoic confidence had drained away with the event of the procession and news of the high priest's actions. They all knew something terrible awaited them and that nothing would be averted by casting some golden object into the still waters of the lake. Something more terrible was going to happen. Some black rite that the gods invented to torture mankind was to be played out on the shores of the lake and people spoke in whispers about the fate of the sun. The sun would be swallowed whole by the moon and mankind would have no protection from the darkness and its fearful lord Tlaloc.

The people and the priests took a broad, easy path to the river. This path was somewhat longer than the track taken by the high priest and the messenger earlier that evening, however progress was good and the priests were certain they would reach the chosen spot at the appointed time.

"If anything startles you my son, run and hide. They will pay you no attention and I think the gods will not take revenge upon you. If the sun is failing go and hide in the earth like they did in the story I told you and help will come to you. If the sun god is to fall out of the sky we need have no fear of the gods, they cannot protect themselves in the face of this calamity. It is nature itself that we should fear and there I have no counsel for you for I do not know what to do. I am sure the high priest will try to appease Quetzalcoatl with blood and I hold out little hope for an answer from the feathered snake. When the end comes it will go badly for our people and they may slay one another. The high priest has shed blood this night."

Treoc's grandmother replied "The priests shed human blood in far off times and in faraway places I have heard this still occurs. The northern sun demands the hearts of men to shine in the sky and the priests in the far north sacrifice their prisoners of war. Our gods have not got the same thirst for human blood. They are different from us and the things we put great store in matter nought to them. Should they choose to destroy each other they would not even see us. We would perish like the trees in a fire, unheeded, left behind by the running masses."

They continued along the road to the lake heavy hearted and uncomfortable. The planets wheeled in the sky and the stars shone fiercely. Not a cloud was in the sky and the air was heavy and unseasonably warm. The air was heavy and still and the priests clanked and made lots of noise as they passed. The procession made its way through the forest, along the path to the shores of the lake where the messenger waited at the lakeside with the silver bowl. The high priest was nowhere to be seen.

The messenger had time to recount all that he had seen to the people in detail and they wondered at the high priest's behaviour. The priests said nothing but the populace were chattering with a mixture of fear and anticipation as the high priest finally emerged from around a hillock, limping along the path to the shores of the lake.

He took the silver bowl from the messenger and unwrapped the silver sickle. He raised his voice and said loudly so that all the people assembled there could hear "We have two days and several hours left before the cataclysm. Once the sun is swallowed by the moon, we have little time to live and devote our energies to supplication and penance. Quetzalcoatl may listen to us but first we must sate his hunger.

The gods demand blood. Blood from llamas, blood from bats, blood from birds. Blood and life as a sacrifice in place of our own. Bring forth the sacrifices!"

The priests in the procession had brought a number of animals with them and at the high priest's request they presented them to him.

The priest slit the animals' throats or killed them by another quick, efficient means one by one. He drained the blood from the corpses into the silver bowl and poured the blood into the water. The blood was warm and the water cold.

The water failed to boil and the priest, although he felt light headed did not experience the euphoria he had expected on performing the sacrifices. The feathered snake remained inscrutable, not uttering a word or venturing a serpentine hiss. The priest pricked his thumb and let the blood drip into the water. He fancied he heard a hissing noise as the blood hit the water and was vindicated. Sacrifice was the way forwards and their only hope of salvation. When animal blood was insufficient for the feathered snake then blood of another kind must be sought out.

He would need all his powers of persuasion and all his priestly influence with the crowd to obtain what he required. He knew that the people teetered on the brink of unbelief things were too quiet, too calm. The night was balmy and the stars shone as brightly as ever.

Faint rays of sunlight shone across the lake. The night was over – seemingly. The sun began to rise as the moon sank and just as the sun began to become visible above the horizon. The paths of the moon and the sun intersected and the feeble light was drowned by the black disc of the moon.

"The first sign of our destruction!" cried the high priest. "The sun is set upon by the moon. Only blood can atone for our crimes. The blood of these animals is not enough to sate the feathered snake only human blood will wake Quetzalcoatl and rescue the sun!"

"Seize the man that brought the crystal bowl to the lake!" commanded the high priest. The priests and acolytes complied. They grabbed the messenger roughly by the arms and dragged him to the high priest. The high priest slit his throat with a flourish of the silver sickle and the messenger's blood gushed into the silver bowl.

"Make good your escape from here" whispered Treoc's father in the boy's ear. "Flee this priest cannot shed enough blood and I fear that we shall be next. You are young enough that they won't chase you they'll think you are too young to know what is going on. We must remain for the moment but run now boy."

Treoc ran to a clump of trees at the edge of the lake and then to a rocky outcrop behind the high priest. There was nowhere further to go on land so the boy slipped quietly into the ice cold water, drew a deep breath and swam out into the depths of the lake.

The high priest poured the man's blood into the waters and the lake sounded as if it boiled. Pleased by the reply he heard from the lake the priest grinned manically and held the silver sickle aloft. The rays of the sun began to reappear from behind the moon as the eclipse passed.

The crowd breathed a sigh of relief.

"Do not be complacent" warned the high priest. "There are more sorrows in store and the world itself will end in two days should we not call on the feathered snake to divert this disaster."

"More blood is called for. How shall we obtain it? Which of you will go to the sun? Choose someone from amongst yourselves and I will send them to the godhead."

Treoc swam for what seemed like an eternity. He swam far out to the middle of the lake and then turned to the north, swimming slowly and steadily. He was tiring now and was looking forward to reaching the north bank of the lake, where he knew there was a path back to the village. A few bold strokes and he was at the north shore. He crawled out of the water and lay on the sand gasping for breath. The surreal events on the eastern shore were far behind him now like a bad dream and he just wanted to sleep and think about nothing. He closed his eyes and lay like one of the dead on the beach.

On the eastern shore of the lake, the crowd were disconcerted. The priest had predicted the end of the world and yet they had lived through a mere blackening of the sun. The sun's warm morning light shone over the lake now and the populace were glad of it. There was something normal and reassuring about the early morning sun. The people stared across the lake at the rising sun and wondered what to do. The sun had disappeared but only for a short time. Perhaps Quetzalcoatl had saved them all. The high priest was a law unto himself and could do as he liked but he had made the people afraid. Human sacrifice was uncommon and electing a sacrifice unprecedented.

"Let us return to the village to think on these matters and reach our decision" said one of the priests. "We have no skill in such matters" said someone in the crowd. "Perhaps Tlaloc is not hungry and the feathered serpent has heard our prayers" said one of the acolytes hopefully.

"We are in a sacred place and a decision must be made now!" commanded the high priest. "I will choose someone if you cannot.

Bring me a draught of elixir and I will see what the gods demand! Am I the only soothsayer to see our destruction?"

"No lord," assured the priests "we have read evil signs in the entrails of our sacrifices and we know that the stars predict ill fortune. The times are very bad and the future of the sun itself is uncertain. It has been swallowed by the moon only to be spat out again but it is perhaps not long before it is consumed again and this time for good."

The high priest took a cup filled with a strong-smelling substance and drained it in one gulp. His eyes rolled back in his head and he threw his head back and let out a gurgling sound. The high priest saw the tongue of the feathered snake flickering in and out and he tried to divine what the hissing might mean. "Treoc, Treoc" hissed the snake. "I want the child Treoc. Where is he?" demanded the high priest.

The priests and acolytes searched the crowd for the boy but could not find any trace of him. This enraged the high priest. "Quetzalcoatl demands the blood of Treoc. You shall offer him to the gods or face total destruction. The mountain smokes and threatens to erupt, the sun will fall once more into the belly of the moon and the stars will fall from the sky leading to our ultimate end in fire and smoky ruin."

"Holy one, he is nowhere to be found" replied one of the acolytes. The high priest over powered the acolyte and proceeded to cut his throat with clinical simplicity. The man's blood coated his hands and his clothes and the stricken acolyte fell to the ground.

This angered the other priests. They had been content to accept the high priest's demand for sacrifice as genuine but this was wanton slaughter of one of their number. One of the elder priests urged the people to go home. "Disperse, leave this place. We face the god's anger all the days of our lives but we need not perish needlessly in mad disputes where no proper sacrifice is made. The high priest is not himself and we cannot wait to be senselessly slaughtered."

The high priest flew into a rage "The earth's doom is at hand. The gods demand blood. This is our only hope of salvation. Do not abandon this place. Your homes lie in the path of destruction the volcano will see the destruction of them all. This is the only safe place I have foreseen it. A few chosen people may survive with the intervention of the feathered snake. You face the gods wrath if you leave."

The people were uncertain. Treoc's relative hurried to leave as did the elder priest and a number of the townsfolk. Most of the people remained. Unwilling or unable to leave. Likewise most of the priests remained at the lakeside, unable to leave in the face of the day's events. "The sun was darkened by the passage of the moon and the omens are bad we cannot leave. The gods will curse us and our destruction will be certain. We must listen to the high priest. The gods are eccentric and demand things that it is hard for humanity to fathom. The high priest is touched by the gods and the very madness of his actions is proof that he is under the influence of the feathered snake.

"Bring the child Treoc to me!" demanded the high priest. "The feathered snake has asked for him by name." The priests and the acolytes protested that the child was not there and they had no way to search for him without leaving the clearing which they had been told not to do.

The high priest appeared to be taken aback and he did not know what to do. He looked at the water and at the bloodied silver bowl and he looked at the body of the dead acolyte. "Was this right?" he thought to himself. The acolyte's death was not a sacrifice, the man's blood had not been caught in the bowl and given to the lake. He was the high priest but he feared the people and perhaps they would find this too much to bear. The best solution was to obey the letter of the god's will. "Bring Treoc to me he will be given to the river. This is not slaughter but ritual sacrifice at the will of the gods. Our salvation is possible but not without bloodshed. Acolytes go and search for the child and bring him back to me here. I will stay with here with the people and the elder priests and we will pray to the gods."

The acolytes made haste to the village where everyone believed the boy must be. After some searching they came to the boy's father's house. They threatened the boy's father and grandmother but they both protested that they had no idea where the child was hiding.

The acolytes took Treoc's father as a captive and returned to the river bank with the man.

The high priest was preaching to the people. Telling them of the feathered snake and the impending doom of the world. He talked of Tlaloc and the sun and the moon and of Chacmool the jaguar good and a hundred other minor deities and spirits. They all danced in the heavens but the timing of their dance had come to be in error and soon the whole of heaven would unravel and spill upon the earth leading to untold ruin and destruction.

Two acolytes brought Hlac, Treoc's father to the high priest. "This man is the boy's father" the acolytes said. The high priest looked at the man distrustfully and said to him. "Where is your son." "Holy one I do not know" replied the man.

The high priest's eyes burned with anger and he took a step nearer the man, sickle in his hand. "The feathered snake demands your son. I have no power in the matter. If you do not tell me where he is I must give you to the river."

"Lord, I cannot I do not know where my son is hiding."

Aware that the crowd's mood had shifted and that the priests thought he was shedding unnecessary blood, the high priest hesitated.

He knew the gods demanded blood and the boy was not to be had. Worried about his control of the crowd he turned to two of the priests who were close counsellors of his and said. Give this man to the river. The gods will accept him from you.

Up until now all of the sacrifices had been made by the high priest himself. The priests were frightened to take the sickle and the bowl from the high priest so they took the man and bound his arms and legs with vines and weighed him down with stones then they took him to a deep place in the river and threw him into the water. He sank and disappeared below the surface.

The high priest was displeased with this compromise. "The gods demand blood and you have cast the man into the lake to drown without shedding any blood for the delight of Quetzalcoatl. This sacrifice does not fulfil the requirements of the gods seek the man's son it is Treoc that we need no other will do."

The acolytes redoubled their efforts to search for Treoc. The day was beginning in earnest now, the sun was higher in the sky and the birds were singing. The people were hungry and agitated and the high priest was conscious of a need to reunite them and to prop up their failing faith in the end of the world.

The high priest decided to leave the edge of the lake and return to the temple. He bade the people go home saying "More sacrifices are required but we are human and need nourishment ourselves. Better to fast and pray but men are weak and our weaknesses are things we often indulge. I bid the priests and acolytes to hunt for the child Treoc and all to reassemble here on the edge of the lake at sunset. When the sun leaves the sky, he should go accompanied by one of our kind."

Treoc woke to the sound of bird chirping. He looked around and recognised the edge of the river and the path leading back to the village. Sensing that people would be hunting him he left the path and climbed some scree that straggled off to the northwest of the lake.

Treoc looked for a sign of human activity but could not find one. This reassured him and he made his way along the slope until he came to some vegetation and plunged into the jungle.

The high priest returned to the temple and consulted the knots on the many tasselled wall hangings in the temple. The knots held all sorts of meaning for the people. Simple communication and more cryptic messages from the divine or from the universe itself were bound up in the sequence of knots on a tassel and the sequence of tassels.

The tassels all spoke of the feathered snake and his abode at the end of the north wind. The feathered snake lived in the north and his hot breath sustained the people.

He thumbed through ambiguous knots and ties with at least two meanings. What was is that Quetzalcoatl wanted?

The knots could be read as predicting great destruction. That much was clear. They talked of destruction of the temple and the sun would go down one last final time. Surely this meant the end of the world?

The temple remained solid and looked resilient and as ageless and severe as ever. The high priest felt tired. What if the end did not come? He had condemned men to death and shed much blood. If the gods were displeased with his sacrifices then they could wreak terrible revenge on the priest and his kin.

His grandfather had told him that in his father's time, the priests had doubted the authority of the high priest and had flung him in the river as a probe of his divine protection. His grandfather had not told him if the priest sank or survived by miraculous or mundane means.

The high priest saw only destruction ahead and should they somehow be saved, he would bear the brunt of the people's unbelief and would be the subject of their impious utterances. Any salvation they could look for surely needed his intervention but he did not count on a grateful reception from his folk should they be saved.

Appeasement was his aim. He ran his hand over the knots on the wall tapestry and got his fingers tangled in an old knotted section of the wall hanging. He pulled at the tapestry to release his fingers and heard a grinding sound like stone against stone. Something was moving behind the tapestry.

He flung himself on the ground and prostrated himself before what he believed was a motion of the god. The room was still. The tapestry fluttered back and forth as a result of agitation by the priest. The high priest could feel cold air flowing from behind the tapestry. After lying motionless for several minutes, he rose and tried to move the tapestry to one side. The wall hanging was fastened to the wall on all four sides and thus it was a difficult task to move the massive wall hanging. He resolved to taking his dagger and sacrilegiously cutting some of the more mundane knots with well known meanings on the right side of the tapestry. He could now stick his arm into the gap between the tapestry and the wall and he felt around blindly until he felt a dislodged stone and felt the cool air on his hand. There was a cave or grotto behind the wall.

This had to be a sign from the feathered snake and this place was obviously some sacred grotto or forgotten chamber of the god. Summoning acolytes, he gave them directions to remove the tapestry without damaging it and to dislodge stones from the wall until it would be possible to crawl into the space behind the existing wall.

The acolytes complied and the tapestry was hastily but respectfully removed from the wall. A stone mason was called as the priests had no idea about how to remove the stones without causing a collapse and work on the excavation was begun.

Meanwhile the high priest examined the obverse side of the tapestry. What truths would he find in these mirrored knots and where the weaving ran in a different direction? The knots here told strange tales. The feathered serpent ate its own tail and was swallowed up. The sun sank beneath the water and it boiled and all creation staggered and fell into ruin. This was just what the priest had predicted. A cataclysmic end to everything. The symbols that he could read and the knots spoke of ending spoke of a time after the gods when there was nothing. Tlaloc the rain god laughed and the resulting storms shook the world.

The high priest was strangely jubilant, this was what he had foreseen. There is splendour in the end of all things he thought. There was a solemn duty in being the last priest. If the gods could not help themselves we were bound for the fire and something greater willed this demise. The whole of nature was tilted to destruction let us not ward ourselves against it but prepare for a fitting end to life, so thought the priest and his black despair lifted.

The opening was scarcely large enough for his head and shoulders. He bade the stone mason continue and retired to his room to meditate on what he had read in the knots and hieroglyphics on the tapestry.

The stone mason laboured gingerly on the stones directly above the hole. He chipped mortar away from between the stones and tugged gently at an outcropping rock. The rock shifted and came away in his hand. He continued to work on another stone. Chip, chip and then pull.

The opening was large enough that a man could stick his head into the opening. The stone mason did not dare to do this however, he called for more light and an acolyte brought him a torch. He held the torch up to the stones and into the cavity. He could see bones beyond the wall. Presumably human skeletons and hints of gold and brightly coloured painting on the far wall of the cavity.

He shivered and took a step back from the work. "This place is accursed!" he cried. He refused to continue to remove the stones until the high priest was called and told about the discovery.

The acolytes were displeased and urged the man to continue with his work. "You might find yourself a sacrifice to the feathered snake" they chided. The man stubbornly refused to do any further work and the acolytes sighed and ran off to seek their master.

The man stayed in the room, keeping his distance from the cavity and the tapestry and he shivered and muttered curses. If the end of the world was nigh he had no mind to meet the angry gods that were to bring it about.

The stone mason thought the end of the world probably was approaching. The sun had been darkened by a celestial body just as the high priest had predicted and so much blood had been spilt. Surely, this would not happen for any reason other than that the gods had gone mad and resolved to destroy the world. He worked out of fear, thinking that the priests might kill him too should he refuse but his hands shook and he hesitated in his work and now that he had resolved to stop, having disturbed a tomb he could give himself wholly to the terror of the future and the cold comfort of an uncertain present.

He knew the legends about the boys that had survived the cataclysm but could see no way to emulate their feat. He was seldom in the mountains unless it was to tread the well-known road to the quarry and thus he had no idea where to find a secret cave or some other shelter from fire from the sky. He had heard the high priest muttering about the end of the world. How Tlaloc laughed and the feathered snake consumed itself. This made him convinced that the tapestry was evil and he shunned it and moved as far from the wall that bore it as he reasonably could.

The acolytes found the high priest prostrate on the floor. He was in a trance and could not be woken. This terrified the acolytes. "He is possessed by Tlaloc!" one cried. "He has entered another world" said another and they fled. The high priest remained on the floor for several minutes. He stirred. He had been in a swoon and had no recollection of how he had come to be on the floor in a trance like state.

Curiosity was paramount. The high priest was anxious to return to the excavation to see what he could see in the newly opened chamber. He hurried to the nook where the tapestry had hung, impatient to be the witness of new portents from the failing gods.

He found the stone mason cowering in a corner and saw the opening in the wall. He ignored the mason and focused his attention on the hole in the wall. He grabbed a torch from the wall, thrust it into the hole and looked with wonder on the contents of the cavern.

He saw a never before seen depiction of the feathered snake on the far wall of the chamber. Depictions of Tlaloc were also to be seen and the general composition spoke of ending. The end of all things. There were skeletons seated in the room. Three long dead men sat in eternal vigil over the picture of Quetzalcoatl and Tlaloc. Their hair and their fingernails still grew although the rest of their bodies had decayed leaving only bones and a foul miasma. Curved knives lay at their feet. Long and sharp and still bright in the torchlight. Armed sentinels kept watch here for some invasion from beyond the grave.

The high priest was a small man. He was slight enough that he could clamber through the hole in the wall into the chamber beyond. Having done so, he was arrested by the friezes on the wall. The feathered snake ate it own tail. Fire belched from the snake's innards and generated a hot wind that blew the rain god's rain and fireballs from the heavens. The very sky was afire as the sun disintegrated and the resulting burning brands made their way to earth. The high priest trod carefully to one of the skeletal protectors of the room. He picked up the knife. It was strangely oily to the touch; probably poisoned with some jungle unguent. He dropped the knife and wiped his hand on his robe. He did not want to be snuffed out by some hundred-year-old poison so close to the time when man might meet the gods and have an ending or perhaps a beginning more terrible and glorious than any imagined in a bygone age.

He made his way carefully to the far wall of the chamber, anxious to inspect the painting in detail. As he crossed the cavern, he trod on a sabre that belonged to one of the long-dead guardians. The blade cut effortlessly through the priest's shoe and buried itself in his foot. He withdrew it immediately but the pain was intense and it seemed that the blade was probably poisoned with some noxious weed or jungle plant.

He was at the far wall and was inspecting the painting of the feathered snake. Astronomical symbols in the left-hand corner of the picture left him cheered. This was to happen in two days' time.

Commotion from the corridor notified the high priest that the acolytes had returned. They reproached the stone mason and made their way to the hole.

The high priest called to them. "Come through the opening. There are things in here that we must all see." One of the acolytes tried to comply. He was bigger than the high priest and his shoulders and torso were too large for the opening. The man pushed and strained at the wall and the stones loosened and collapsed burying him and trapping the high priest in the cavern.

The high priest searched about the cavern seemingly in vain for a second opening and a potential way out of the cave. He eventually found one, to the right of one of the guardians he could feel a cool breeze and there was a cave in which he could walk upright.

He followed the cave limping and cursing seemingly for hours on end until he came to the mouth of a river. He crossed the river and bathed his wounded foot. On the far bank of the river he could see some light. The tunnel was coming to an end and he would soon be outside again. He snapped the fresh air and anticipated his return to the outside world.

The things he had seen in the cavern had reassured him that the end of the world was coming. Perhaps it would come before he expired from his wound, which was very painful. He emerged from the tunnel into dense vegetation and he was scratched and aggravated as he made his way out into a clearing.

He had no idea where he was. He was in a densely forested valley with few landmarks for him to get his bearings. He could not be far from the temple but there was nothing familiar about the valley. He took a guess that the temple was to the East and headed in that direction, limping badly along the narrow clearing in the forest.

The stone mason attempted to free the trapped man from the rubble but by the time they had dug his head and shoulders free, the man was dead. The acolytes wanted to continue to excavate in the hope of freeing the high priest but the mason refused to help.

"Evil tidings come from this cavern and I have no wish to encounter more ill fortune. The high priest is surely dead if the cavern collapsed. Choose a new representative for the feathered snake and let us find some way to avert the coming catastrophe."

The acolytes ignored the man and continued blindly to shift stones and dig in the rubble. The stone mason took the opportunity to flee and left the temple and went to a distant relative's house in the town. He had no wish to be recalled to deal with a second collapse. "Maybe the mad priest is right and it will rain fire from the sky tomorrow" complained the stone mason to his relative. "The things I have seen today make me think the luck has all run out."

His relative replied "We must find a way to take shelter like the boys in the old stories. There are many caves and hidden dales around this place and some of these are sacred to the gods. There is hope for survival if you know where to go. Perhaps we should flee to safety this very night. The omens are bad, of that there is no doubt."

The stone mason agreed and they packed what little they could and made their way into the mountains on the way to a cave that was known to the stone mason's relative Feri.

The high priest stumbled onto the shores of the lake. He was at a spot somewhat to the north of the place where he had sacrificed and he knew now in general which way to take. His foot made the way difficult but he was determined.

He came across a small boy picking berries from a tree. "Child! Return to the village. These times are grave and you should not be out and about alone" exclaimed the priest.

Treoc ran at the priest's urging. He was fortunate that the high priest had not recognised him. He ran until he reached a fork in the path and then took the path that led to higher ground. He ran straight into the stone mason and his relative. The men recognised the boy from the events at the lake and invited him to join them in their safe haven in the mountains. Treoc accepted when he heard that the stone mason had abandoned the high priest and the party made their way hastily to a cave in the hills.

The high priest took the lower fork in the path that led back to the far shore of the lake. He was in agony and could only hobble slowly along the rocky way. He reached the shore where the sacrifices had been made and threw himself down on the sand. The acolytes and the people would return to this spot when it grew dark. He had not long to wait.

The acolytes in the temple believed that the high priest was buried in the cavern beyond the temple wall. They scraped and dug frantically to reopen the hole between the two rooms but excavation just led to further collapse of the remaining wall stones. Eventually the acolytes broke through the wall. The cavern beyond was empty except for the skeletal sentinels and the acolytes realized that the high priest must have escaped.

The most enterprising of the acolytes was called Xlita and he now decided that they should proceed to the shores of the lake as planned. The end of the world approached and they had best be ready for it.

Xlita doubted that an end to all things was coming. Such cataclysms were cyclical and although the wrought great destruction, man usually survived somehow. His personal survival occupied a great deal of Xlita's attention. He was disturbed by the high priest's penchant for human sacrifice and thought that this was something that would not interest a god. The gods were inscrutable and not really interested in the affairs of men in Xlita's opinion, the sacrifices that they seemed to like consisted not so much of human flesh and blood but of bright baubles and strangely carved stones. They were not like us. Of that Xlita was sure.

He chose not to take the silver bowl and the sickle with him when the acolytes left the temple. Enough blood had been shed. The sun would be swallowed or not regardless of what men did. All they could do was watch and wait and perhaps hide in the earth. Had he been less important, XLita would have hidden in the mountains. As it was his presence was demanded and he made his way with grim resolution to the shores of the lake.

They did not expect the high priest to be waiting for them at the lakeside. The high priest sat on the sand near the water and gave loud sullen orders to the assembling acolytes. The priests would have much to do on this night.

"Blood is demanded. I myself have been cut open by the will of the gods and my life bleeds slowly away beyond any help. Sacrifice and supplication are our only hope of survival."

"Bring me the silver bowl and the silver sickle. Let them be awash with blood!"

The priests hurriedly sent someone to the temple to retrieve the sacred implements Xlita asked the high priest if he should find someone to examine his foot.

"I hold out little hope that I may be cured." Replied the high priest "but I should stand for the rites that we are about to conduct. Bring a healer from the village."

Xlita made haste to the village. Here he sought out an old woman wise in herbs and plants. "The high priest's foot has been grazed by a poisoned blade and we know not what to do." He told her.

"He has the madness of the angry gods" said the woman "I may fail if I try to heal him."

"Come bring your witchery with you and attempt something. There will be no one left to bring you account should you fail. Our lord prophesises the end of all things."

The old woman assented and they left for the lake shore. Xlita had to go at the old woman's pace and it took them a long time to reach the shore.

The high priest sat and waited in a feverish trance. The people had begun to assemble to see what would happen to the sun. If he would again be swallowed by the moon?

The wise woman examined the high priest's foot. "Salt to draw out the poison and then coriander for the swelling." She rubbed salt in the high priest's wound causing him visible pain and then bound the wound with a cloth. The high priest found a long stick and found that he could stand with the help of it.

"The sun will soon be devoured!" shrieked the high priest. "Our time is at an end. Abase yourselves before the gods." Some of the people fell to their knees, the rest quaked with fear and gasped. The sun continued on his leisurely journey into the west.

More and more people were coming from the village. The lakeside was crowded and the people waited to see what the priests would do.

Most of the priests did nothing at all, being content to watch and attend the high priest. They were not certain if the high priest spoke in a fever or if he communed with the gods and spoke of things beyond their ken.

"The feathered snake swallows his own tail. Tlaloc drowns in the rain! The gods themselves will be no more and all will be darkness or primal fire."

"Bring the boy to me! I commanded that he be taken for sacrifice this morning. Acolytes where is he?"

"We do not know high priest, fled into the jungle or the mountains and we cannot find him."

"Tlaloc desires blood! Choose, choose from amongst yourselves who is to be sacrificed!"

The people were aghast. One man cried "The end of the world comes not. The sun is secure on his path into the west and he has not been swallowed by the moon. The priest is mad and wills us all to an unnecessary death!"

The high priest flew into a rage. "Seize the blasphemer he will go to the gods to explain his churlishness."

Xlita nodded to the acolytes and they seized the man and brought him to the high priest. They held the man firmly and the high priest slit his throat with the silver sickle and caught some of the blood in a silver bowl. He poured the blood onto the water and exhorted the gods to drink deeply.

The people were stunned into silence. The sun continued on his path into the west unconcerned. The high priest was also unconcerned by the sun's continued survival.

"The sun remains on his path while he is buoyed by the blood we have shed. Our sacrifices have stayed the gods hand and they debate what to do. Destruction remains assured but we have the attention of the gods. I plan to pray for clemency."

"The sun is doomed. We will be a people in darkness." As he spoke, the sun sank below the horizon perhaps he will not rise again."

"The blood I have shed is our bargain with the gods. Perhaps should they survive they would make man anew if they think he will do their bidding and provided them with pleasing gifts. This is not the first time the world has come to an end. There are many times when the sun has fallen from the sky. This time is special because I foresee an end to the old gods. Tlaloc and Quetzalcoatl themselves fight for life and seem caught in a fatalistic struggle against self-annihilation.

The blood we have shed has had an effect. The sun has trod his weary path again and remains secure in the sky. We feel the hot breath of the feathered snake in the wind. The gods continue to live and have us to thank for it. This blood keeps them alive. When the gods themselves perish we can expect only our own destruction and the whole collapse of the natural world. Further sacrifice is required if we are to hold the gods back from annihilation and if we are to preserved the sun on his perilous journey across the heavens.

Things are not as they once were. You saw yesterday the omens where the sun was swallowed by the moon. Fire and destruction will surely follow. Feel the hot wind, hear the rumblings of thunder and the mutterings of the angry gods. Our destruction is still almost a surety. The feathered snake gnaws his own tail, Tlaloc commands so much rain that he himself will drown. How much hot water from the sky can we endure? A hot rain will fall that can boil your blood and we will have fire from the sky."

Sweat dripped from the high priest's forehead and his features were contorted with pain. Xlita thought he spoke in delirium but knew better than to say so. Xlita feared the crowd and had no idea what they would do to the priests if the high priest was not in control so he tolerated the mad situation.

As if on cue large hot rain drops began to fall from the sky. The high priest felt as if these caused small burns to his flesh and he cried out. "Tlaloc will unleash so much rain that he himself will drown."

The rain made the assembled people think of seeking shelter an idea which even the high priest seemed to grasp. He told the acolytes to return to the temple and limped resolutely after them, leaning on his stick.

The rain intensified and the people were soaked to the skin. This was yet to show signs of being a flood but the omens were bad enough that the people were prepared to believe this was the second catastrophe in the series of events that might lead to the end of the world.

The sun had not been swallowed today. Perhaps the gods heard men and had managed to change their inscrutable fortunes. Perhaps as the high priest said the gods were debating their fate and the blood spilt had focused their attention on humanity for a brief instant, giving them a temporary respite – perhaps time to run and hide.

In the cave Treoc and his companions heard the rain patter on the roof of the cave. Strange for this time of year, the rain nevertheless gave Treoc a sort of comfort. He had been expecting molten lava – fire from the sky as the priest had predicted. Rain was a much more benevolent event. They had settled into the cave and Treoc had eaten some boiled beans that the stone mason's relative had given him. Treoc's life had changed dramatically in the course of a day. His father had been killed before his very eyes and he had fled from the village, which was the only place he had ever known. The stone mason and his relative had never had business with his father so Treoc hardly knew them.

Perhaps he and his two companions would be the only people to survive the cataclysmic end of the world and they would emerge from their cave to find a wholly new world, empty of humanity and all signs of civilisation. His eyelids felt heavy and he threw himself onto the ground to sleep.

During the journey to the temple Xlita brooded darkly on the uncertain future. Human sacrifice had never been a part of their religion until the high priest had demanded and carried it out. The people were terrified, replacing the high priest meant a religious and power vacuum which Xlita thought would destroy society. Convincing the high priest with new auspicious omens that the disaster had somehow been avoided was all that Xlita could think of doing. Should the disaster be real then there was little help in worrying about it but the sun's steady path into the west had shaken Xlita's faith in the omens.

Dissent had shaken the high priest's faith in his ability to lead. A man had openly professed doubt in the signs of the gods. The high priest had killed him but the people's doubt was something he could ill afford. The high priest was convinced the end was nigh. Human survival depended on divine supplication. His ancestor who had been drowned set an unwelcome precedent for his replacement but more than personal fear, rather a deep despair in the future dominated the high priest's feelings. Whatever the people sought to achieve, the high priest believed they faced certain destruction with any other leader. He was pessimistic enough to think that they might try to overthrow him. He knew he had demanded things that they were reluctant to give and that their faith in the astronomical events heralding the world's end had been shaken. He wondered if this temporal problem might be part of a greater cosmic problem where all authority becomes unseated and chaos reigns in the spiritual and temporal realms. The gods themselves were uncertain of their fate.

He could hardly expect to remain firmly in charge when all were in the grip of panic and despair.

He hoped that the signs from the natural world and the spectacle of sacrifice would imprint on the people's minds the importance of what he did, that they would somehow understand that the gods were mad for blood and sustenance and that the old powers of nature have been put to the test resulting in a world poised on the brink of destruction. He hoped they would understand that the very principle of life was required by dying gods.

These were the things he had to make clear to them. They poured out blood for dying gods. The deities they had worshipped for centuries were coming to the end of their lifespan. The sun was feeble and old and the moon threatened to swallow him up.

Most of the acolytes were frightened by the prospect of the end of the world, being fervent believers in the feathered snake and in Tlaloc and they were prepared to do the high priest's bidding even when it seemed abhorrent. This was not a normal time and the rules of everyday life were somehow suspended. A few of the acolytes who followed for the most part Xlita were more circumspect about the approaching end of the world. They followed Xlita's lead and as he was resigned to the sacrifices they made no move to oppose them. Perhaps they hoped for a new high priest. The high priest was wounded and had proclaimed that his very life's blood ran out.

The people were scared. Whether convinced of the approaching end of the world or sunk into scepticism they were frightened of the high priest. Surely the man did no wrong or the gods would instantly punish him? However, what they demanded was fearsome and unprecedented. Some of the people doubted that the end of the world was approaching. The days came and went as before and although the temporary disappearance of the sun was discomforting they saw no end in sight. The high priest was mad but they were too frightened to do anything. The priests were to be obeyed and that was that. Many thought of flight either to be safe from the cataclysm or to escape the high priest's attention. A return to the village was welcome and from there they would go to hide in the hills.

The rain intensified and everyone made their way home. The high priest was soon back in the temple. Desiring to see the new image of Quetzalcoatl, he went to the collapsed wall and bade the acolytes to dig further. His wound troubled him and he had limped home, with a burning sensation in his foot and leg.

The rain drops were unusually large and hot. The water collected and pooled around the village and the temple. The sky was black and foreboding and lightning flashed and thunder crashed over the village and in the mountains. The top of the temple was struck by lightning – an omen that was not lost on the high priest. Tlaloc was clearly angry. They needed stone masons and builders to help them clear the stones away so that the hidden chamber could be reopened. The high priest sent acolytes into the town to round up any men they thought were suitable. The stone mason who had disappeared was widely regarded as the best in the village but there were other men with skill in stone work.

The men came reluctantly to the temple and began their work. They shifted stones tentatively and left many standing that the acolytes would have removed. This was however they claimed essential to avoid a further collapse. The high priest was unhappy with the slow progress and urged the men to excavate more quickly.

The rain continued to fall and lightning and thunder lashed the mountains. Treoc and his companions heard the thunder and wondered if it was the start of the end of the world. This storm was more intense than any other they had ever lived through.

In the village, the streets were muddy and the villagers had to walk through ankle-deep water. The rain showed no signs of abating and they wondered about the possibility of a flood. The high priest brooded on this possibility as well. A flood might be their means of annihilation. Legends of great floods were known and they involved great loss of life.

Perhaps the gods had chosen this means to be rid of humanity. If only he could read the symbols that accompanied the painting of the feathered snake in the recently collapsed chamber. He was certain that they contained information of relevance to the end of the world. The high priest thought that his excavation was perhaps the most important thing he could currently do. Further sacrifices were difficult at present though he did not doubt that they were what the gods desired.

The builders made more progress than the priests had and there were no further collapses. Eventually they opened a passage to the previously hidden chamber. The men did not like this work. They made signs of to ward off evil and muttered amongst themselves that the priests must be mad. The high priest was delighted that the men had made an opening into the hidden chamber and he urged them on.

"Quetzalcoatl wills it that we uncover his image. There are important sigils written on the wall. I will read them to know better the mind of the feathered snake in the face of the present catastrophe."

The men said "Holy one we are frightened that the feathered snake will swallow us. Let us desist with this digging and leave this place. It is accursed."

Faced with such open superstition and disquiet on the part of ordinary people the high priest was taken aback. He did not want to provoke them and lose his hold on the populace. "Make the hole large enough for a man to crawl through and you may go.

"We want to go for our homes are threatened by flood. Perhaps we shall be engulfed holy one. Let us go and save ourselves in the hills."

"Go and fly from the wrath of the gods. You have my blessing I doubt that you will be spared for I foresee the destruction of all things but go and make an attempt to preserve yourselves and your families. Sacrifice to the gods, corn or chickens or whatever is fitting. The gods demand sacrifice and do not hold their hands back from destroying us."

He let the men go and called an acolyte to help him clamber into the chamber once more and another to bring him an old codex that he thought would be of use in deciphering the message of the fresco in the cave.

Outside, the rain came down in sheets drenching everything and collecting in rivulets on the streets. The water was as high as a man's knee and the village was overcome by flood water. The people gathered what they could and made their way to higher ground, soaked to the skin by the hot relentless water.

Water started to trickle into Treoc's cave. The water doused their fire and the stone mason cursed. They made to move to higher ground deeper in the cavern but the men were afraid that their exit would be cut off by the water.

"Perhaps we have simply found a new death here in what was meant to be our sanctuary." Complained the stone mason.

This disquieting thought disturbed Treoc greatly and he scurried into a high and dry part of the cave. He thought of his grandmother and of the animals penned near his home. He wondered what his grandmother was doing and if she had let the animals go. They had little hope in the storm. The people in the village would have to scramble now to get to higher ground and find somewhere dry to take shelter from the flood.

The flood waters had deepened and the village was waist-deep in water. Meanwhile the high priest was deep in his grimoire comparing passages with patterns around the fresco. "The feathered snake swallows his own tail. He sees the very end of himself." He read. "When Quetzalcoatl eats himself where will the wind blow from? His hot breath will not set the clouds in motion anymore and there will be no respite for anyone on the earth. The old god dies and the world goes on without him hail the old gods! Men shall offer something fitting at their passing so that they do not go forgotten into the dark like the unremembered shades of men long dead."

This writing confirmed what the high priest thought. The gods themselves were dying and humanity could look for a world turned upside down as a result. There was more written on the wall. A strange description that meant little to the priest. The writing read "I am in the cavern with teeth above the lake where the paths all come to an end." He knew he had to mediate on these words to understand what Quetzalcoatl's scribe meant by them.

The water was becoming a problem in the temple as well. The entrance was muddied and was knee deep in water and the priests were unsure if they should leave the temple and head for higher ground or if it was their duty to remain and brave the flood. Xlita went to consult the high priest.

"I am troubled by a prophecy I cannot understand" said the high priest. "We must stay here and meditate on the meaning of the words in the cavern. Drowning in water may be our doom but then so let it come to pass. We will not fair better no matter how far we run" he said when Xlita asked him about the flood.

Xlita though that the prophecy referred to a place but he kept his thoughts to himself. The high priest was, he believed, mad and he had no wish to exacerbate the madness by setting him off in search of a new treasure. He might slay someone for religious purposes or out of some pious response to a misread shrine inscription. Xlita felt that enough blood had been shed but he dreaded taking the reins of power and knew that deposing the high priest meant chaos and more deaths for his people. Better a mad high priest, one touched by the gods than a mountebank come to the office through bloodshed and treachery.

Xlita was however a curious man and he could not resist sending someone after the mysteries in the cavern. He chose a young acolyte and told him. "Make your way to the river and then climb into the hills till all paths disappear and try to find a cave with stalactites like teeth. The first part of your journey will be wet but in the mountains, you will fare better than us. Go and when the flood subsides return and tell me what you have found."

The errand boy sped away from the temple, wading in the deep water until he disappeared in the direction of the lake.

Treoc, the stone mason and their companion were miserable and wet in the cave. The water had stopped rising quickly but the rain continued and everything they owned was wet. Treoc moved into a part of the cavern where only he could stand and was startled by a golden snake. The snake did not move and when Treoc looked closely he discerned wings on the serpents back made from a clear glassy material. This was an image of Quetzalcoatl and there were strange inscriptions carved into the sides of the snake.

Treoc told his companions what he had found and they made the sign to ward off evil. "Some shrines are evil and not all holy places are safe for humans. Leave the golden thing alone and stay well away from it. This is something for the priests and not for ordinary folk."

"As soon as the weather improves, we must move to another cave" said the stone mason. "If such a move is possible, the water might keep coming till the end of the world."

The stone mason's relative laughed nervously. Treoc left his corner and returned to the centre of the cave where the men stood in the water, their packs on their back and their faces pinched with worry.

Tlaloc said "Do men make such things or are they artifices of the gods themselves. I do not think any man in our village has the skill with metal to make such a thing as this feathered snake."

The stone mason drew breath and said. "There was a time when the arts of men were more highly developed than they now are. There was masonry done a hundred years ago which we now cannot do. This is the work of men but we have kept no record of our achievements and the secrets of our artifice were not passed on from father to son. I think the men of the past had many talents which we have lost and that they had a dedication to their crafts which we sometimes lack."

"They say in the past that the weather was better and the sun was stronger and the people were richer and had lots of shells from the sea. "continued the mason's companion.

Treoc asked "Could we not rediscover these arts in the present?"

"Some men seek to do this or to discover new things in their arts that were hitherto unknown. The stone masons trade is a good one for someone so curious. Arrow making is a traditional business with little room for improvisation or improvement."

Treoc laughed. His father had always said that people who did not make arrows like he did, exactly as he had been taught by his grandfather made them the wrong way and they would never hit their mark or penetrate a beast's hide. "Arrow makers follow a traditional trade but they are not always traditional people. My father did not want to give me up to the high priest for sacrifice." he said.

The water continued to collect in the cave, making Treoc and his two companions uncomfortable.

The high priest meditated in the temple. A sacrifice was required to mitigate the rain god. Tlaloc was a fearsome god not lightly to be invoked. The high priest resolved to send men to the village to take prisoners for sacrifice. He would perform the sacrifice here, in the temple. The high priest made his way to the living quarters within the temple. These were empty and partially under water. The priest realized that he had been in a trance and had not noticed the encroachment of the flood. He sought out the temple walls. A few sullen priests stood on the temple wall in the lashing rain.

The high priest implored them to go into the village and seize the first person that they should meet and bring them to the temple.

"Lord the people have fled the village and we doubt that we will find anyone there." Replied one of the priests.

"Go nevertheless Tlaloc demands that you provide him with supplicants."

Three of the priests departed for the town. The going was difficult, the water came up to their waists and they doubted they would find anyone in the village. On coming to the village, they found an old man sitting on the roof of a flooded house. They took him by force to the temple. He was unwilling to leave his home and remonstrated bitterly with the acolytes that took him away.

He came before the high priest who said "Are you ready to meet Tlaloc the rain god?"

The man answered "Rain falls from the sky as it will the gods have little to do with it I hope merely that the flood will subside and I can return to my home. The world will not end in a flood. You told us that fire would rain from heaven and all we have is water."

"Impudent unbeliever!" cried the priest. Explain yourself to Tlaloc and the high priest slit his throat with a silver dagger and had an acolyte catch the gushing blood in a silver bowl. The high priest commanded that the blood be poured out on the roof of the temple as an offering to Tlaloc. The frightened priests obliged.

As they left the high priest's presence they muttered amongst themselves. "The old one tells the truth. The end of the world has not come, this is merely a flood." Others said "The water is high and it may come to pass that all things are drowned or float away. The end may come in a way unlooked for as the high priest himself struggles with the finer points of the prophecy as they are detailed in the images of Quetzalcoatl and written in the knots."

The high priest mused on the phrase "where all paths come to an end" surely this meant that Quetzalcoatl had come to the end of his path and he would consume himself. The high priest thought this interpretation fit with the predicted end of all things. He sighed. "What is the use in sacrifice if such a disaster cannot be avoided?" he asked himself. However, they had rain instead of fire in the sky, perhaps the gods had heard him and accepted the sacrifices. If the end of the world did not come, he did not know what to do. Were they then to be sustained by constant blood sacrifice or could they revert to the old ways and offer up chickens and corn to the gods?

He feared that they would require a constant supply of blood. The priests obeyed him now, now that they thought the end was nigh but in an ordinary time would they be prepared to herd the people to him for slaughter? These temporal problems vexed the high priest. He was conscious of the acolytes' hesitation and their uncertainty when it came to obeying his commands. Should they openly rebel it meant his certain death and then perhaps the destruction of the people when the sacrifices were neglected.

These things depended on the end of the world being somehow averted and the high priest was far from certain that this was at all possible. He just knew what the gods demanded or rather some of the things that they demanded. Some prophecies remained unclear to him.

He decided to consult the knots. A series of knots on the tapestry remained unread and he would fain read them. He looked at them carefully, a long sequence of small and large knots. There was sacred meaning hidden here, things forgotten and secrets never uttered out loud.

His foot continued to worry him and he sat on the floor as he examined the knots, his legs crossed and massaged his wounded foot. The wound felt hot to the touch and he had a burning sensation in his leg.

"I have come to the end" he read "to a place where the feathered snake reigns supreme. Where the other gods are cast down and there is nothing else." This seemed to indicate war in the heavens that perhaps Tlaloc and Quetzalcoatl would war with each other – a war of the wind and the rain. Tlaloc was a dark god who meant men no good. Quetzalcoatl on the other hand was something of a luck bringer. A victory for Quetzalcoatl was good news for mankind.

"There is nothing else." Repeated the priest to himself. What did the end mean for humanity? Did it mean fire from heaven and excruciating pain leading to death and oblivion or did it mean that everything would just suddenly stop? There would be no further warnings, just the end. Perhaps that was Quetzalcoatl's promise an eternal sleep rather than a slow punishment leading to grisly death. The snake swallowed its own tail. That was it thought the high priest the terror of being consumed alive. That was what the feathered snake would do to the world. Humans could just remain small a small part of nature in the face of such a catastrophe.

Was sacrifice necessary to avert the end of the world or was it part of the end? The high priest thought that perhaps it was the latter. He had been driven to such extravagant and bloodthirsty rituals by visions of the end of the very gods but this was also a sign of their weakness, depending on humanity for survival rather than being above and beyond it and not open to appeals any more than the wind or the rain respond to a man. He wondered if people would escape by hiding in the earth. He knew the legends of the old fathers of men well, how they had hidden in the earth in a time of cataclysm and emerged to start a new civilization. Nothing was in the knots to indicate that there would be survivors this time around. He did not know if the survival story had been prophesised in a previous era by the priests of Tlaloc or Quetzalcoatl or by the servants of the sun.

He thought it would be wise to find out and called to an acolyte to bring him the tapestry describing the survival story.

The acolyte brought it to him and they leant over it to examine the knots and tassels that trailed from it. For a long time, they could not make out anything new in the story. When the earth was threatened with destruction some people fled to a cave and survived when all else was destroyed. There was little new to read into the story until the very end where they read "and the gods so willed that these people survived to worship them."

Thus, human survival was intended but when the feathered snake consumed himself who was left to be worshipped? A new sun and a new god of the winds? Also, humanity survived to do the bidding of the gods and to sacrifice to them.

This gave the high priest pause for thought. He needed followers that could perform the sacrificial rite. Then they would be destined for survival. Up until now, the high priest had performed the sacrifices himself. He needed to convince his acolytes and at least some of the people to spill human blood for the gods as he himself was doing. Then their survival was at least a possibility.

The people had fled the village and were hiding in the hills and caves around about. Finding them would be a difficult task. The high priest resolved to do this himself. As he was injured, he needed a litter to carry him above the waist high waters. Four acolytes were assigned to the task of carrying the high priest. Everyone hoped this would become easier as the litter left the village and was carried onto higher ground. The reality was that the men nearly drowned keeping the high priest upright on the litter. The high priest suffered many jolts and bumps and the jarring did his injured foot no good.

They climbed into the foothills around the village and at a loss for where to seek the people, they headed for higher ground. The trees thinned and the ground became stonier. The rain blurred the surroundings and rivulets of water rushed quickly downhill everywhere. There were no caves in sight and no signs of human life.

The high priest bade the acolytes to put down the litter. He got up and limped around in the rain. He began to chant softly "beh

beh hara beh". He pointed to the east. "We must go that way." He said. He returned to the litter and the acolytes bore him once more. Eventually the came to a rocky outcropping under which a number of people were sheltering.

"Quetzalcoatl calls on you to do him homage!" cried the high priest. "It is not just the priests that must make an offering. To save yourselves you must shed blood!"

He gave his sickle to a woman in the crowd. "Now cut someone down with it!" he cried! An old woman cackled and said something to the younger one with the sickle. The younger woman grit her teeth and slit the old woman's throat.

The other people in the group recoiled in terror and moved away from the young woman. She looked at the high priest as if asking him what she should do.

The priest gingerly took the sickle out of the woman's hand and he praised her saying "Perhaps you shall be chosen for salvation, go and hide yourselves in the belly of the earth!" The people fled and the priest was left alone with his acolytes, the young woman and the body of the old woman.

"Holy one," said the woman, "I did your bidding and now the people are afraid of me. I am frightened of going into a cavern with these people in case they should avenge this woman's death by killing me. Where must I go to find shelter?"

"I will send you to the temple. There are caves and tunnels beneath and behind it and perhaps there you will be safe or it might be that there are no safe places with the coming end of the world." The high priest sent an acolyte with the woman with instructions to take her to the temple and to keep watch over her.

The high priest continued to search the hills for several hours for the villagers with little success. Eventually they came to the mouth of a cave. Smoke issued from the cave, making them sure that there were people within. The high priest dismounted his litter and hobbled into the cave on foot.

A group of ragged farmers from the village greeted him. He exhorted them to take up the knife and slay someone in a ritual killing but they said to him "master you are our priest. We do not understand these things and cannot perform rituals. This would be mere murder in our hands."

The priest did not know what to do. "You are doomed!" he shouted, "Quetzalcoatl will not save you from ruin. The end of the world is your end as well. I shudder to go into the dark and meet the gods. You will do so without making an offering and the gods doubtless be displeased when you come before them."

At this the people quailed and were afraid. Everyone refused the offer of the sickle but still they lived in fear of the end of the world. They did not know what to do and they huddled closer to the fire, unsure of who they feared more the mad high priest or Quetzalcoatl the insane god consuming himself alive.

The high priest despaired of stirring the farmers in the cave into any sort of pious slaughter and he left them to shiver before their smoky fire and returned to his litter.

He drove the acolytes on, fretful to encounter more villagers. They came to a stone hut in the mountains. The rain slewed off them in torrents and the ground was a muddy, squelching morass.

An old man and an old woman lived in the hut. As there were only two people in the hut and as he thought they were too old and frail to be saved, the high priest slit their throats.

"Come we must seek our people" said the high priest. The acolytes pressed on, glad to be away from the site of the slaughter. The rain pelted down relentlessly and the high priest and the acolytes were wet and miserably hot. The land was large and they had many places to look. Many of the villagers would probably remain unfound.

They came upon a dozen villagers sheltering under a rocky outcrop. The high priest exhorted them to take up the sickle and offer a human sacrifice to Tlaloc and Quetzalcoatl but they were too timid to take up his challenge.

"Lord," they said, "we will only bring the gods' curse down upon us more swiftly and more deeply if we kill. Ordinary folk are we and we do not feel the power of the god calling us to slaughter as a chosen one like you must feel. We are afraid and value our lives even though they soon may end. We can do nothing against you and you are our overlord by custom, rite and law."

The high priest despaired. "You are all surely doomed. Quetzalcoatl swallows his own tail and the sky has grown black. The sun is uncertain on his path through the sky and will soon be extinguished. Fly if you can, flee to the deep places of the earth. The gods have woeful things in store for us. Sacrifice is what they demand. We are pitiful things compared to the gods. Which of you can shake the clouds and make the thunder roll like Tlaloc?"

"Holy one," they replied "we fear the gods and the coming end of the world. We would escape it if we could and hide from the wrath of the gods. We will do as you say and find a deep cave to hide in."

"Tlaloc and Quetzalcoatl will find you! You will drown in the waters that attend the end of the world or live to be sacrificed on the altars of those that the gods have chosen!"

The high priest let them go. He was disheartened and frustrated with the people. He knew that the end of the world was inevitable. In the face of such a serious event all that went before was turned on its head and new ways and new laws were required.

"I will find others willing to do Quetzalcoatl's bidding" he said to himself. The party pressed on. The ground became steeper and the litter was difficult for the acolytes to carry. The high priest was perched precariously on the litter and held on for dear life.

They found another party of refugees from the village. Miserable and wet underneath a tree. When he exhorted them to make a sacrifice, a man sprang up and took the sickle and cut down one of his comrades. He brandished it and used it a second time, slitting the throat of a shocked onlooker.

He made to attack one of the acolytes but the four acolytes worked together and overpowered him. "Let this one be sent to the temple!" commanded the high priest. The acolytes were reluctant to let the man go. "He attacked us, the holy ones he has no sense of our special dedication to the gods" one of the acolytes said.

"This man understands something new" replied the high priest. "The gods yearn for blood and demand sacrifice. No blood is too precious for them. I have shed my own blood for the god. Perhaps a sacrifice may come from amongst the priesthood yet. However, I agree that we are the chosen messengers of the gods and deserve the people's respect. Go with this man to the temple, guard him closely. He may be maddened by Tlaloc but he is not profane. He has done Quetzalcoatl's bidding here."

Two of the acolytes departed with the man in the direction of the temple. There were now only two to carry the litter and the high priest was a heavy burden. The three priests pressed on with grim determination through the rain.

They met scattered groups of people but nobody followed the high priest's exhortation to kill. The high priest, frustrated and cold and with a lamed leg decided to return to the temple and to make the most of his existing converts to slaughter. The way back was fraught with peril. They were too few to keep the litter aloft in some of the places where they had climbed up the mountain and the high priest had to limp and stagger as best he could. Eventually, they made their way back to the temple, through the rain and flood waters.

In the temple, the acolytes awaited the high priest. Xlita awaited them. He was deeply disturbed when the chosen two people had arrived in the temple. He was not sure whether to treat them courteously but with care as important prisoners or to have them executed. Their behaviour alarmed him and it spoke against the natural order in Xlita's opinion. If anyone could make such a blood sacrifice, the role of the priests would be devalued to say nothing of the grisly, unnecessary nature of the sacrifice itself thought Xlita.

Knowing they were sent to the temple at the behest of the high priest, Xlita had opted for courtesy until now. He was really hoping for an order for their imprisonment or execution. None such order was forthcoming. "These two shall be the salvation of our race!" cried the high priest.

At this moment Xlita's emissary in the hills chanced upon a cave with teeth-like stalactites. He cautiously entered the cave and became aware of two men and a boy sheltering in it.

As he approached them they shook with fear. Thinking he had come to kill them. The acolyte however asked them if there was anything unusual about the cave. If they thought it was haunted or given to the gods.

The stone mason (for the three were Treoc, the stone mason and his relative) replied. "Yes. The cave has some evil to it. There are strange offerings to the gods here. This boy found an image of Quetzalcoatl in an alcove."

Treoc pointed to the alcove where he had found the golden and glass snake. The acolyte got on his hands and knees and crawled into the space. He was amazed at what he found. "Leave it where it is." Hissed the stonemason.

The acolyte complied. "Xlita and the high priest must know of this and they will doubtless want to come to this cavern. I must hasten back to the temple. Leave this place if you can. Do not disturb it further."

"We must shelter somehow from the rain." Exclaimed the mason's relative.

Treoc felt relieved when the acolyte left the cave. He had not recognised any of them as he was someone from the temple who seldom came into town and thus Treoc was fortunate not to be recognised and delivered up for sacrifice.

"We must leave" said the stone mason. "Perhaps we can find another cavern where the air is not foul and there are no sacred objects or witch symbols." They decided to explore the cave further and found an opening leading down to a now flooded rivulet. The stone mason waded in and was in water up almost to his chin before he came to the other side, which appeared to be large and inviting.

They made their way across the rivulet and into the dark recesses of the cave. The stone mason managed to light a torch and they looked around them into the inky blackness of the cave. Nothing was to be seen except for the rocky walls of the cave and the stalactites from the ceiling. This reassured the stone mason. A dark hole was preferable to somewhere accursed or to a holy place – such places were not for men in his mind.

The rain sounded distant, fainter in this part of the cave. Treoc wondered if perhaps the storm was becoming less severe. He was pleased that they had light and some warmth now and it was certainly drier in this part of the cave.

The messenger sped on his way back to the temple. He reached the temple without difficulty and proceeded to find Xlita. As he sought him, he came upon the high priest.

"Messenger what news?" asked the high priest. "We have found an image of Quetzalcoatl in a cave far from here." Replied the acolyte. "The place is surely holy to the feathered snake. Two men and a boy had taken shelter there. I instructed them to leave. Such a holy thing should not be profaned."

The high priest was delighted that a sign had been sent by Quetzalcoatl. "Quetzalcoatl's image is an important sign from the gods. We should sacrifice before it and make the god an offering of blood. I will go to the cave if you will lead the way but first I must see to the new acolytes, who will be the special messengers of the gods."

The acolyte knelt before the high priest and then left to change his wet cloak for dry clothing. He knew he must still deliver his message to Xlita but he was sure that Xlita would be pleased that the high priest had taken an interest in his journey to the cave.

He changed his cloak and exchanged words with some of the younger acolytes. They told him of the strange pair that was under guard in the temple and warned him that Xlita was displeased.

Eventually, the acolyte found Xlita and made his report. "Everywhere the high priest sees signs of ruin and decay and our greatest works make him hungry only for sacrifice and death." Sighed Xlita.

To the acolyte he said "I will go with the high priest when he journeys to the cave. This is an important discovery. You have done well."

The high priest went to that part of the temple where the man and the woman who had killed were being held. He welcomed them to the temple and had the acolytes bring them food. "You are to become the new priest and priestess of the angry gods. You must placate them with blood and sacrifice. This is how we will survive, when the sun is fed with blood and the feathered snake smells death on the wind." The priest sang to them. He sang a long lay about Quetzalcoatl and his interaction with humanity.

Then he instructed the pair in certain rituals that the priests carry out. He had the plant brought that gave visions when it was smoked and they smoked the leaves of it.

The woman questioned him "Are we prisoners here?" He answered "You are under guard but that does not mean you are imprisoned. Demand what you will, the guards will bring it to you. You are the new priestess of Quetzacoatl and black Tlaloc. You will be treated reverently."

He instructed the guards to do what the pair asked and then took his leave of them.

"A relic of the feathered snake has been discovered and I must see this thing myself." He said.

The high priest sought out some acolytes to bear him to the mountain and found the messenger who was to show them the way. They set out in haste from the temple. Even the high priest realized that the rain was not as heavy as it had been and that the flood waters were subsiding.

This cheered the acolytes no end. They said to each other maybe Tlaloc and Quetzalcoatl have relented and we will all be spared.

The high priest said "The end is nigh. Water will be replaced with fire from heaven and we will perish except perhaps for the new priest and priestess. They will do the gods proper homage unlike you timid acolytes."

In the cave, the wind blew on the stone mason's torch and it was guttered. The torch flickered for a while and then went out, leaving Treoc and his companions in darkness.

This boded ill for the trio. They sighed and waited to see what the darkness would bring.

The high priest's litter climbed the mountain with less trouble than earlier in the afternoon. The messenger guided them along the twisted path that lead to the cave with stalactital teeth. The high priest cried out at the sight of the cave mouth. "This is a fitting resting place for the feathered snake! Here we shall find portents of Quetzalcoatl." The priest foamed at the mouth and uttered strange syllables "gar nac ah"

Treoc and the others heard the high priests cry echo from within the cave. They knew their only hope was to remain still and hope they were not detected on the other side of the river from the cave's treasure.

The high priest alighted from the litter and limped into the cave entrance. The messenger lit a torch and followed him. "Holy one, it is here." He said and pointed to the alcove containing the simulacrum of Quetzalcoatl. The high priest stumbled forwards and then reached out for the messenger's arm to steady himself. They bent low to enter the alcove and as the torch was thrust into the darkness of the alcove golden light was reflected from the stunning treasure it contained.

"We must carry this to the shores of the lake." Commanded the high priest. The acolytes had made their way into the cave and were dazzled by the beauty of the feathered snake all wrought with gold and gems and glass.

The men were afraid to touch the feathered snake. The high priest handled the object, which was too heavy for him to lift. When nothing appeared to happen to the high priest, the men were reassured. "Take hold of the statue" he commanded.

Four acolytes grabbed the corners of the statue and succeeded in lifting it out of the alcove and into the wider space at the cave entrance. "Bring it out into the open" ordered the high priest. The acolytes successfully hoisted the statue out of the cave and into the open woodland beyond.

Here a dilemma became apparent as they could no longer bear the high priest's litter, occupied as they were with carrying the statue.

The high priest ordered two acolytes to remain with the statue and had the remaining two carry his litter. The messenger went ahead of them with instructions to bring two more helpers to bear away this precious cargo.

The high priest instructed the acolytes chosen to remain with the effigy to bear it to the lakeside. He would return to the temple and lead an entourage from there to the lake. A great sacrifice was to take place at the lake and the high priest foretold that there would be a rain of fire from the sky.

Two heavily burdened acolytes bore the litter back down the mountainside. The high priest had another fit and foamed and frothed at the mouth. He said that the feathered snake would consume them all and that only sacrifice delayed their inevitable demise. The rain had slowed but it still made going difficult and the treacherous paths in the mountains meant that it took the acolytes an hour to negotiate the path back to the temple.

At the temple, the high priest gathered all of the acolytes and servants together. He told them to make ready to depart for the lakeshore at the earliest opportunity. He spoke to the man and the woman that he had sent to the temple earlier in the day. He gave them sickles and brass bowls and urged them to prepare themselves mentally to become instruments of the gods.

"I know who belongs to Quetzalcoatl!" cried the woman. "The feathered snake will feast on their blood tonight."

"Good!" exclaimed the high priest "sacrifice is demanded by the gods. If you feel their lust for human blood you can serve them like few others."

The two under guard were accompanied to the lake shore. The high priest rode in his litter to the lake.

The rain was definitely subsiding. The high priest's litter made good time and they were soon at the lakeside.

The party that had been sent to transport the statue soon arrived and the four acolytes shifted the heavy artwork tentatively. They were fearful of a curse of the gods and took pains that no jolts or harm came to the image. Their way was torturous and long with many halts and pauses. They often had to think of an alternative route or stop and wait for the rain to subside.

Treoc, the stonemason and his cousin were still in the cave. They had heard shouting when a party of acolytes arrived but no one had entered the cave. "They have taken the idol." said the stonemason. "Surely they have brought the gods curse down upon themselves with this foolishness such things are not for mortal men."

They thought to leave the riverbank and seek a place that was more comfortable and safer. They recrossed the river and entered the larger cavern. "Now that the idol is gone this place disturbs me less" said the stonemason.

They returned to the cavern, it was drier now and here they were able to light a torch and have some light and heat. "I think the high priest's men have gone for good." Said the stonemason. Treoc breathed a sigh of relief. The rain was easing and perhaps the cataclysm had been and was gone?

At the lakeside, the acolytes, the high priest his new favoured couple and Xlita were assembled. The high priest bade messengers to go and rouse the people. Everyone was to come to the lake.

The rain had definitely abated. The high priest took this as a sign of further catastrophes to come.

They waited staring at the lake surface as it was pocked by the rain. The high priest started to sing. A chant that became melodic and throaty at the same time. The acolytes joined him in song. It was an invocation of the feathered snake. Calling on Quetzalcoatl to make the wind blow.

The wind did blow. The wind blew strongly from the west. The high priest chanted and wailed and he rattled a rattle at the west wind. He began to writhe like a snake and to shiver.

He was suddenly silent as if listening to the wind and the acolytes also stopped chanting. He shivered and raised his arms in the air trembling all the while.

"Water will be replaced by fire! The wind will rouse a fire and the fire will descend from the sky and the flames will engulf us all."

The rain stopped and the wind blew a gail. The rain stopped with these words from the high priest and the acolytes shook in terror.

"Wooo" wailed the wind. "Sah" chanted the acolytes in terror.

The woman took her knife and cried "Oh Quetzalcoatl I deliver a sacrifice unto you!" She slit the throat of an onlooker, an old man in the crowd and caught his blood in a silver bowl. The blood she took and poured over the high priest.

The high priest licked his lips and tasted the blood. He limped to the water's edge and bathed fully clothed in the waters that ran red around him.

"Such is the demand of the gods. That we sacrifice of our own to them. Quetzalcoatl and Tlaloc have mighty anger great enough to shake the world from its foundation and spell our downfall for all time."

"Few will be spared. Perhaps none. Do what pleases the god and offer sacrifice!" commanded the high priest.

"Fire will rain from the sky and the earth will shake! The stars will fall from the sky and the sun will be disrupted from his path through the heavens."

The high priest began to wail like the wind "woah woah" he moaned.

The woman washed herself in the water of the lake in imitation of the high priest and she too made noises like the wailing wind.

The acolytes chanted "Sah sah" and the people shook in terror. More people were coming to the lake as the weather gradually improved and as the acolytes found groups of stragglers in the hills. They came to the water's edge as they knew not what else to do.

The four acolytes charged with carrying the statue of Quetzalcoatl toiled through the wet scrub and vegetation. There was a substantial journey to the lakeside and they had to often stop to rest.

As the rain rolled away a rainbow became apparent and in the cloudy distance lightning flashed and thunder rolled.

The thunder cracked solemnly in tempo with the high priest's song and the people cowered in terror.

Treoc, the stonemason and his cousin were aware that the rain had stopped. The thrumming on the cave roof had come to an end and the water everywhere was subsiding. The stone mason suggested "We should try and find another cave. Anywhere is better than this god-accursed hole." Treoc and the other man agreed. They made their way to the entrance, peered cautiously out into the jungle, fearing that the acolytes were still nearby and finally stepped cautiously out into the open. The loud thunder gave the stonemason to understand that the storm might return and they hastened to find another shelter.

This was achieved with some difficulty. They skirted around the craggy hills and sought, if possible, a cave to hide themselves in. They eventually found a low-ceilinged crevice and made their way to the back of this scooped out hillock. This was less comfortable than their previous cave dwelling and they resolved to seek another in the morning. Treoc was reassured now that there was more light and less rain and he began to hope that they might see another person and perhaps be spared the end of the world.

The stonemason resolved to press on after they had spent about an hour cowering under the rocky outcrop. The storm had abated and he thought they might find a better shelter. Treoc was apprehensive, having found a new shelter, he felt they should wait for a sign that the cataclysm was over but just what this might be he was not sure. Perhaps a comet or the flight of a strange bird or some other unusual event.

He thought of the old stories, where the heroes received messages by strange means. A pattern made by falling raindrops or a sandstorm that left a city in its wake, the strange call of the whale.

The stonemason was adamant however, they must move and find some more permanent shelter. He was not convinced that the danger be it supernatural or man-made would soon pass. He was aware that travelling overland would expose them to the danger of discovery by the high priest's minions but he believed that they would be occupied with the idol and the important sacrifices they would no doubt make to it. What danger other groups of people might pose he did not like to consider. The desperation which drove them to flee was great and they might not like being discovered by even his poor party.

They would be easily discovered where they were. The cave was easy to see into as it was too shallow to be dark and indeed was more a scooped-out rock formation. He knew the boy was loathe to go out into the rain and wind in the search for an uncertain haven.

Nonetheless Treoc followed the stonemason and his relative out of the cave and into the rain. The forest was quiet except for the rhythmic patter of the falling rain and the hum of myriad small insects. They were heading downwards into more populous and more densely forested regions away from the barren mountain crags that had hidden them so well.

They were following a path now that led steadily down towards the settled valley. They were apprehensive and fearful of discovery. A twig snapped on the path ahead of the stone mason and he instinctively started. A guinea pig appeared and they all relaxed. The stone mason's relative loosed an arrow and killed the animal and they rejoiced at the opportunity to eat fresh meat.

The stone mason took the guinea pig, skinned it and placed the carcass carefully in his satchel. They continued along the path and came to another overhanging rock. Here they stopped, the stone mason made a fire and they jubilantly cooked the guinea pig. Treoc could not remember when he had last so enjoyed a meal. The stone mason also became cheerful and sang a nonsense song that made the boy laugh. The stone mason's relative played his flute and they forgot about their troubles for a short while.

Then the stonemason became aware of the need to press on. He kicked sand on the fire and urged Treoc and the other man to move on. They made haste to get on the road and followed the path ever downwards, towards, if only they had realized it, the lake.

The path became broader and easier to traverse and the vegetation retreated. The flood waters were not fully in retreat here and they had to be careful about the route that they took or they would be cut off by the flood.

They came to a point where the road was completely submerged and were forced to double back. They struck out on a path perpendicular to the road. This led through dense vegetation and was hard going for Treoc. The men slashed at vines and branches and eventually they made their way to a clearing.

In the clearing there appeared to be another path leading deep into the jungle. They followed the path deep into the jungle where the light was blocked out by the trees. They made their way into the deep jungle and were grateful for the protection of the trees. A snake crossed their path and they thought that perhaps this was a sign from the feathered snake.

"Perhaps the feathered snake wants us to follow." Whispered Treoc. They followed the snake through the undergrowth and the thickly wooded area.

The stone mason cursed and muttered to himself. He saw the snake as a bad omen but felt he had no choice but to follow it on its winding journey through the undergrowth.

The snake devoured a mouse in its path and the party wondered about the significance of this event.

"The high priest would see this as a sign for sacrifice." Said the stonemason. He took some grain from his satchel and sprinkled it on the ground as an offering. "I hope this is all the gods require of us." said the stonemason. "From time immemorial it was animal blood and corn that we offered to the gods. Our own blood is something they would not take and the priests of old would have found it profane to offer."

Treoc was reassured. When the stonemason spoke of sacrifice he had been scared that the men would turn on him. He was well aware that he was earmarked as a sacrifice to Tlaloc by the high priest and that they might actually carry this sacrifice out if they caught him. He was relieved to be going more deeply into the jungle and away from populated areas.

The branches hung low and the men had to crawl. Treoc was hunched over like a cripple as they sidled along in the dense foliage. The snake still in their sights with a disturbing bulge in the otherwise cylindrical body.

They came to a running stream and the snake slithered alongside it and into a small hole. They looked around and discovered that they were at the mouth of a cave.

They entered the cave with some hesitation (Quetzalcoatl is normally no friend of man). The cave floor was wet with puddles of water everywhere and they knew they had little hope of making a fire. The cave was dark and they wondered where the snake had gone.

Eventually, the stone mason found a dry shelf of rock at the far side of the cave where they could attempt to light a fire. They managed a smoky blaze with wet wood. Treoc's eyes hurt with the smoke and he was not convinced that they were better off in their new hiding place. At least the walls were bare and there were no evil paintings or idols to contend with.

The stonemason's relative started to sing an old song to cheer them. He sang about the corn harvest and they all breathed a sigh of relief. This was a festive song one that was sung when all were sated and in a state of relaxation.

The acolytes dragged and pushed the statue through the undergrowth and onto the path that led to the lake. Considerable effort was required to get the idol moving and there were many stops and starts. The men were naturally mortified if it looked like the delicate glass might be shattered or that one of the finer veins of gold might be bent. They were naturally more than agitated when the idol tumbled down a steep section of the path, rolling over onto the wings. The precious glasswork held preserved as if by some supernatural agency from destruction.

They managed with considerable effort to right the statue and resume carrying it carefully down the well-trodden, sodden path to the lake. The vegetation thinned and the lake became apparent in the distance. They redoubled their efforts, aware that the high priest waited impatiently for their appearance with an intact idol at the lakeside. Several of the acolytes believed the idol to be accursed and blew upon their hands to chase the evil away. They held the idol gingerly, afraid of catching some horrible disease by profaning the sacred object.

To one of the acolytes however the idol was nothing but dull gold and sharp glass. Litl was a favourite of Xlita and was known for his originality of thought and for strange behaviour in general. He did not like such hard, physical labour – the acolytes generally did not do so much fetching and carrying and to be one devoted to the gods was to have certain privileges amongst the people. Litl knew full well that the blood crazed high priest would not take kindly to a damaged idol and thus he also handled the statue with care.

He secretly believed the high priest had gone mad. The end of the world would surely not come just from rain and a darkening of the sky. He also doubted that the gods wanted blood. He believed they were inscrutable and took little interest in the affairs of men. Hence the wildness of the world and the harsh days that men had to live through. Litl thought that the gods had better things to do. Plotting a course for the stars and steering the sun safely through the heavens.

This idol was, he was convinced the work of some long-dead master craftsman here on earth and not something that fell from the sky. Things occasionally fell from the sky. He had seen the rock that fell to earth, leaving a vast crater in the soil. The heavenly messenger was not in the least anthropomorphic and any message it carried from the gods was not to be easily read. Displeasure undoubtedly to hurl such a rock at the earth.

Perhaps the gods were frustrated with earthly imperfection. The earth was such a half-formed chaotic place in contrast with the heavens where the stars moved in their slow, graceful dance. Litl thought they simply had better things to attend to than the paltry affairs of men and the minutae of the jungle.

There was still a long way to travel down to the lake below. He hitched his side of the statue up high In the air and proceeded to make the best of it.

At the lakeside the high priest was making a fiery oration, describing the end of the world in vivid detail. "Fire will fall from heaven. Flames will engulf us. The mountains will spew forth hot ash, lava and poisonous ether that will choke us and burn. The earth will shudder, earthquakes will abound and the land beneath the village will be torn asunder. The temple will fall and lightning will strike the pinnacle. When the rain ceases, we are doomed. Repent of your crimes before the gods sacrifice and do penance for the offences you have committed in the eyes of Quetzalcoatl and Tlaloc!"

"Blood is demanded, blood and the beating heart of the sacrificial victim should be placed on the idol of Quetzalcoatl. When the idol arrives there will be sacrifice and the gods will shake the heavens with delight. The end of our world does not necessarily mean and end to all our people. The gods will reward those that do them proper homage and sacrifice in the prescribed manner. Those that shed blood for Quetzalcoatl may yet be saved to do the gods homage in a new world."

The high priest cast a significant look at the woman and the man that he had chosen from the people. They were his hope for a new nation of people to serve the gods after the cataclysmic end of the world.

"We come here to sacrifice and then you must flee and hide in the deep places of the earth for there will be no shelter on the surface of the earth. Nowhere will be safe from the hot winds that Quetzalcoatl blows with fiery breath. Deep in the earth a mother and father will sire a race that serve the gods with fresh blood. Then the sun shall right his course and our civilization shall rise from the ash."

"Today is the third day", he continued, "the third day of the end of the world. Three days ago I saw a vision of the worlds end. After the sky was blackened in the middle of the day and the great flood came, my vision contained fire from heaven and hot lava gushed from the ground. This will be the way in which our world ends. The gods are angry and are not to be lightly appeased. Sacrifice and prayer are their requirements these must be offered to Quetzalcoatl and Tlaloc."

"Quetzalcoatl is the feathered snake the bringer of winds, Tlaloc is a rain god he looks like a human but has the power over rain and thunder and a temper like a wild tornado. The two gods will tear the heavens to pieces and scatter them over the earth. Not content with wrecking the sun's path through the heavens they will cast fire on the earth and burn all that is green to blackened cinders. Hot winds will blow and the heat will be fierce enough to burn everything up."

They heard a peal of thunder. "Tlaloc passes by and his stride is the thunder!" exclaimed the high priest.

This was indeed the third day since the high priest had fallen into a fit and had had his vision of heavenly and earthly destruction. Much has happened in the space of three days and the people are confused and exhausted by coping with mayhem, disaster and the great unknown. Just as the high priest predicted, there was an obscuring of the sun in the middle of the day. Disturbing as it was that the sun, their life-giving source of heat and light would vanish from the heavens, the ensuing flood had done more material damage, destroying their homes and causing loss of life and general discomfort. The prospect of molten lava and fire from the sky was a frightening one indeed and many believed that the end of the world was in fact nigh.

They feared for themselves and their kinsfolk. No one wanted to die in the cataclysm but then neither were they willing victims in the high priest's sacrificial rites. The high priest scared and enthralled them and most were totally confused about the new turn that their religion had taken. They quaked with fear lest they be taken for sacrifice yet some thought the sacrifice necessary with the same reasoning as the high priest, that the gods would be appeased with blood. They were on the foreshore of the lake as far away from the high priest and the acolytes as they could respectfully be.

Xlita was well aware of their fear and agitation. The high priest on the other hand seemed to think that their fears corresponded with his own: the destruction of the world. That they might fear him as an agent of death never crossed the high priest's mind. The high priest commanded and the people obeyed. That was the nature of theocracy and the high priest was so gripped by his visions that he paid little attention to what was going on around him.

Xlita saw the flood waters subside and believed that life was getting back to normal. His challenge was to rein in his insane master and to dispose of the priest's dangerous new followers. The slaughter sickened Xlita and he was convinced that the gods didn't care enough about mankind to seek its destruction. Xlita knew that the idol was coming and hoped this would distract the high priest. He wanted his acolytes to be ready to overpower the couple that the high priest had ordained as the acolytes of a future generation of blood sacrificers.

This pair disturbed him. They had taken the high priest's message to heart and acted on it with bloody remorseless slaughter. Xlita believed the high priest could be controlled, terrible as he was as he was enthralled by portents and signs from the heavens. Xlita hoped the high priest would see some sign or observe some event that would see the end of the end of the world and a resumption of normality. Xlita was aware that the high priest might have to be overthrown, something he was not sure that he could accomplish. Better times were hopefully ahead mused Xlita, times when he could use his influence over the acolytes and the people. At the moment they were too scared and too scarred by the events of the last three days to pay him much heed or to think clearly.

Should the high priest's promised fire from heaven fail to arrive, Xlita would be in a position to act. For the moment he could only watch and wait and try to gauge the mood of the people and his own men.

The men bearing the idol were negotiating a steep descent into the lakeside valley. This was especially difficult with the heavy statue in their possession and they had to stop frequently. They eventually made their way down to the lake shore where the crowd were assembled.

The high priest was delighted that the idol had arrived. "Quetzalcoatl has sent us a sign!" he exclaimed. The idol was a simulacrum of the feathered snake god Quetzalcoatl. The snake's body was golden and the idol had wings of finely detailed glass where one could see the snake's feathers.

The people were awestruck by this sudden apparition. Most of the images of Quetzalcoatl that they had were two dimensional and this lifelike representation worked a great effect on them.

Treoc and his friends were attempting to keep dry and warm in their cave. The rain had abated but there was still a lot of water around and all of the kindling that they had for the fire was wet. This made maintaining a blaze challenging. The stone mason however was in good spirits. "This cave is a wholesome place.", said the stonemason. "No harm will come to us here and we can wait out the storm and whatever worse things are to come." Treoc shivered but said nothing and the stonemason's relative was also silent.

There was a vacant space between the people and the high priest and his acolytes, who stood near the newly arrived idol. The priest began to chant "Quetzal coatl Quetzal coatl." He shuddered with some meditative effort and seemed oblivious to what was going on around him. He hissed like a snake and made undulating movements. He took his knife and pricked his finger and smeared the blood on the idol.

The late afternoon sun lanced through the clouds and shone on the idol. The crowd gasped. This was most probably a sign from the god. The sun was restored to them and the clouds had cleared somewhat. The sun had been blackened in the middle of the day and hidden by the clouds during the subsequent rain. The high priest had said that the sun would be thrown off his course and there would be fire in heaven. The burnished gold of the idol shone like fire and the people were awestruck and somewhat afraid.

"The sun requires blood and a beating heart in sacrifice.", intoned the priest. "Quetzalcoatl will not be merciful. The light of the sun heralds the approach of fires from heaven and we will all be destroyed. There is hope only for those who sacrifice as required by the gods."

His two special acolytes looked restive. "We will perform the sacrifice" said the woman who had killed. She lunged at the spectators who took a step backward. A frail old man did not move as quickly as the rest of the people. The woman snatched him up by the arm and drew her dagger across his throat. He let out a gargled scream. The woman took her knife and cut deeply into his chest, retrieving his bloody beating heart. She ran with the heart to the idol and placed the heart at the idols feet.

"Such is the worship Quetzalcoatl requires!" exclaimed the high priest. "I am pleased with my acolyte."

The clouds parted and the sunlight streamed onto the lakeside.

The high priest built a fire at the base of the idol, lit the fire and threw the heart onto it. The organ sizzled and popped as it was seared by the flames. A smell of burning flesh rose, filling the crowd with terror.

The high priest breathed in the acrid smoke and coughed. He turned around and around and chanted strange words unknown to the populace.

Xlita was sickened and disturbed by the display. The new acolytes were far too powerful. Instead of being prisoners under guard they were the high priest's favoured helpers in his rites of slaughter and death. Xlita suspected that the woman was simply bloodthirsty and craved a long-planned revenge on the people in general and all of those who had wronged her over the years.

He did not know what to do. The crowd's reaction to the arrival of the idol and the emerging sunlight made Xlita think that they trusted and believed the high priest, making any move he might make to overpower the two acolytes dangerous. The high priest could easily demand his blood at this stage and he had no doubt that his two henchmen would be willing to shed it. Xlita was relying on the natural superiority of the acolytes and their personal loyalty to him to tip the scales in his favour and to hopefully lead to an opportunity to end the slaughter.

Eventually, Xlita thought the high priest's prophecies would have to go awry and then the citizens would feel doubt. Xlita would use this opportunity to take charge. The high priest would remain as a figurehead. Someone Xlita could drug and manipulate and the sacrifices would cease. The two he would execute. It was too dangerous to have the common people taking on religious roles. Particularly roles of ritual slaughter. For as long as events seemed to coincide with the high priest's predictions Xlita would have to bide his time. Unless things became untenable and the high priest started to look for sacrificial victims from among the acolytes and priests.

Then, Xlita would lead a revolt. Fire did not immediately fall from the sky but the people were awed and cowed into submission by the bloody acts of the two and the high priest. It was late afternoon on the third day since the high priest had had his vision of the end of the world.

The end of the world that was the high priest's theme now. He emerged from rambling nonsense and whirling about and shouted that the end of the world was inevitable. "The world has ended three times before now and we are at the end of the fourth age. This time the very skies will be torn and heaven will be rent asunder. Fire will rain upon the earth and all things will wither and perish. What was not destroyed by flood will be destroyed by fire and molten rock. The gods are angry. Their anger is deep and has gnawed Quetzalcoatl's belly for long and led Tlaloc to make the heavens shake with thunder and lightning."

"The feathered snake will blow a hot wind that will ignite the furnaces of the sun and then fire will rain down upon the earth. The sun is weak and totters on his path. He will fall from the sky and it will spell ruin for the earth. Go and hide deep under the earth. Even so you will not escape in the world to come the very sun will depend on blood to rise each day and not a day will pass without a heart burning on the altar. The people will war upon another and take captives with the purpose of keeping the sun alive. For we all fall to ruin when he perishes. You know what little remains of the previous ages of the world, when men hid in terror in the bowels of the earth. Their lives alone were all they saved and all their artifice and great works perished as did the animals and plants that kept them alive."

The high priest started to chant, his eyes rolled back in his head and he entered a trance-like state. The acolytes took up his chant. Some with more pious intent than others. Even Xlita was caught up in the chant. From force of habit and the sobering words the high priest had just spoken.

The people, lulled by the sounds of the priests joined in and the whole populace invoked the feathered snake. Perhaps Quetzalcoatl would give them a sign.

The sky shone a dull red colour but the promised fire from heaven failed to fall to Xlita's great relief. He wondered how long the people would be in thrall of the high priest.

The high priest was insensible to all of the activity around him. In a trance, he chattered and sung for Quetzalcoatl.

Treoc and his companions debated what would happen to the world outside. "The high priest predicted the eclipse, which led to the flood and he claimed that the flood would be followed with fire from heaven."

"Hence the necessity to remain safely below ground." said the stone mason's relative. "We should remain here until at least three days have passed."

"If no fire comes from heaven we will starve here below ground in the cold without a fire.", replied the stonemason.

"You are always the superstitious one.", replied his relative. "Whenever we find a spur of the gods you look for the evil eye. A rain of Lava is perhaps best survived well below ground and near water. Perhaps we shouldn't have left the other cave even with the high priest's men about. Now however we certainly need to stay put."

"I disagree.", retorted the stone mason "I intend to hunt guinea pig in the forest now that the rain has stopped. I will go quickly and return with something for us to eat. We will stay the night in the cave and if the fire has not come by morning we can chance returning to the village. Although I do not know what will become of our young friend. He is marked for sacrifice by the high priest and perhaps it is better for him to remain hidden. We can argue about such things in the morning."

"Take me with you!" pleaded the boy. The stone mason looked at Treoc and smiled. "Come let us brave the end of the world for a good dinner."

Treoc was fearful but at the same time he was fascinated by the phenomenon of fire from the sky. He thought that they might quickly have a look and then flee back to the cave hopefully with something eat. His stomach growled and he looked forward to any sort of repast.

They hurried to the cavemouth and stepped out into the jungle. The sun shone in between the gaps in the foliage and the jungle was steamy after the rain. The ground was turned over mud and flotsam and the going was difficult. Treoc sank in the mud up to his knees. The sky remained clear however and there was no sign of fire in the sky.

The stone mason was relieved and set to the task of catching some food. Treoc struggled on in the wake of the man. They heard a twig snap and the stone mason nocked an arrow into his bow. With a great deal of commotion, three acolytes emerged from the undergrowth.

"You will come with us.". they said. They were armed and the stonemason saw no course of action but to comply.

"All villagers are to assemble by the lake to witness the solemn rites of sacrifice that will attend the end of the world.", said an acolyte.

They took the stone mason's bow and his long knife and made the mason and Treoc march in front of them along the steep way down to the lakeside.

"These two are merely frightened peasants." Said one of the captors. "No I believe they are something more.", said the acolyte who appeared to be in charge. "This boy has an aura about him. He is tied up in some business with the gods. Xlita will want to see him."

Treoc was alarmed. There was a distinct possibility that the headman had half remembered him as the chose sacrificial victim. He could not imagine a worse fate at the moment than being delivered to the priests.

The stone mason sensed his distress and laid a comforting hand on his shoulder. "These people do not know us." He whispered. "Say nothing and they will remain in the dark as to your identity and the purpose the high priest had for you."

"What did you say?" demanded the lead acolyte. "I merely asked the boy if he still had any food.", replied the stonemason.

"You lie!" cried the acolyte. "Bind him and the boy so they cannot use their hands."

The acolytes bound Treoc's hands together with a cord. They went to secure the stonemason's bonds and the man proceeded to struggle, occupying two of the guards.

"Run!" commanded the stonemason.

Treoc ran stumbling and righting himself with both of his tied together hands. He vanished quickly into the forest leaving the stone mason behind with the three acolytes.

"Search for the boy!" he heard the chief acolyte cry in the distance. "He is important and my lord Xlita or the high priest himself will surely ask about this one. I remember now the lad is marked for sacrifice. He is the due of the dark god Tlaloc and his blood will be spilt at the high priest's command. It will go ill with us if we fail to provide such a prize to our betters."

Treoc ran until he came to a jagged rock that he judged sharp enough to cut through the cord. He sawed the rope against the rock for some time and eventually managed to free his hands. He needed desperately to make his way back to the cave now. The acolytes were searching for him in the jungle and the stonemason had been taken prisoner. He climbed ever higher over rocks and fels and wherever possible through the densest part of the jungle, hoping to throw off pursuit.

The stonemason was overpowered by his captors. They bound his feet as well and carried him like a hunting trophy between two of the acolytes. "We should return to the lakeside.", said one of the men. "Better if we say nothing of the one that got away. The priests will have interest in our captive. Let them be content with that."

"It will go badly for us if the high priest finds out we let one escape.", replied the man holding his feet. The acolyte in charge sighed. "You two. Take him to the lakeside and I will continue to search here above alone.

The two men departed with the stone mason and made their way to the lakeside.

At the lakeside, the chanting had abated. The high priest was still lost in his own world singing strange words and making wild gestures.

Xlita was immediately aware of the new arrival, bound and suspended between two men as he was. He gestured to the two men that they should approach and they brought their captive to Xlita and dumped him at the priest's feet.

"This man ignored the high priest's commands and fled into the hills.", said one of the acolytes. "Where is Anuik?" asked Xlita, naming the acolyte who had taken charge in the jungle. "Lord he hunts after stragglers and other men of this one's ilk.", they said kicking the stonemason for emphasis.

"You had better go and find him. All of the acolytes should be present here at the lakeside. Momentous things are afoot and your presence is required to observe them and to keep the peace here." He said these last words more quietly but with an unmistakeable emphasis.

Anuik was moderately intelligent and Xlita desperately needed support from those few acolytes that could think for themselves. Xlita was worried that the high priest or his new acolytes would attack the priesthood and sacrifice a priest or an acolyte to Quetzalcoatl in a moment of bloodthirsty madness.

In Xlita's mind it was vitally important that the distinction between the priests and the people be kept rigidly and he was most distressed by the new acolytes the high priest had ordained. Most people were born into the priesthood and that was the way Xlita intended it to remain.

The high priest saw signs and visions that convinced him that the world was turned upside down and that there was a need for new ways and new strength in the priesthood to face the coming tides of destruction. The high priest lived in a world of visions and supernatural visitations he was often in a trancelike state and took little notice of the world around him being focused on the coming end of the world and the rain of fire from the sky.

Xlita was frightened that the high priest might turn his attention to the captive that lay at his feet so he got two of the acolytes to drag the man to the edge of the beach away from the idol, the high priest and the crowd and behind where the acolytes were standing.

He decided to interrogate the man. "Why did you flee instead of obeying the high priest's command to attend the sacrifice here at the side of the lake?"

"We were not informed holy one.", replied the stonemason. "I was hunting in the hills when your men set upon me."

"You said we are there others still hidden in the jungle."

"No my lord I meant only me."

Xlita doubted this very much. He kicked the man and said "Your very life hangs in the balance here and you could easily be delivered to the high priest for sacrifice. Do not lie to me I want to know what is happening in the jungle."

"I am the only one" continued the stonemason. Xlita gave up questioning the man and turned to the acolytes that had delivered him up. "Were there others?" he asked.

Nervously the pair affirmed that they had found a second person but had been unable to capture them.

Xlita pretended to be angry. He scolded the men and said that they were lucky that the high priest had not found out that they had misplaced a prisoner.

"Return to the mountains and scour the hills for this missing boy." Xita commanded. "Do not return until he is found."

More than anything Xlita hoped that the high priest would not focus his attention on the new captives so he thought that sending the men off on a wild chase after the missing boy was his best hope of keeping them away from the high priest.

He would attend to the stone mason. The last thing he needed was for the high priest to take another sacrificial victim. Especially a well-known and influential man like the stonemason.

The two acolytes hastened back to the jungle and decided to search initially for their missing leader and then to focus on finding the boy. They were fearful of Xlita's wrath and did not want to come to the attention of the high priest. The heart at the base of the idol could have easily been one of their own and they did not want to come too close to the blood spattered new acolytes of the high priest. The sudden elevation of these common people to the priesthood and their blood thirsty ways unsettled the acolytes. This was not the way of things, not even at the end of the world.

Treoc made his way through the jungle back to the cave he had shared with the stonemason and the other man. The stone mason's relative was still there and was distressed to hear about the stonemason's capture. They discussed the incident and decided to stay put as neither of them could overpower the acolytes and they dared not venture out in the open. They tried to build a small fire but the tinder would not light as it was too wet. The man sang a song to comfort the boy and they fell asleep.

Xlita wondered what to do with the stonemason. The man had a superstitious fear of the gods and of the priests who served them and he seemed uncomfortable at the sight of the idol. Xlita knew the man had helped at the excavation in the temple and had been successful in opening the passage to the cavern. He was skilled and knowledgeable when it came to stone and there were very few men like the stonemason in the village.

In other circumstances he would have been inclined to befriend the man. Xlita was interested in the art of construction and in how the temples were built. As it was he was obliged to deal harshly with the man and to find out at all costs where his friends might be hiding.

He did not want to attract the high priest's attention. The high priest was in a sort of trance and chanted nonsense rhymes in front of the idol. The people's attention was fixed on the high priest and his new acolytes. Xlita decided to identify the stonemason's companions by a process of elimination.

He got an acolyte to go through the crowd asking after the stonemason's relatives and workmates. He was sure he would soon find out who was absent and then he would be able to efficiently hunt for the fugitives.

Many people were missing but they could well be casualties of the flood mused Xlita. The acolyte recited the names of the missing to Xlita – most of them were people he did not know and those that he did were old and frail, probable victims of the flood. Some members of the stonemason's family had been accounted for but the acolyte was unsure exactly who was related to whom and there was much confusion amongst the people themselves. The acolyte had been told not to accost the people in case this woke the high priest from his ritual trance. That meant he could not cajole or threaten the crowd and was dependent on their confused replies to his enquiries.

He hazarded a guess that the stonemason would be easily gulled by clever words and spoke. "I have heard the names of those to be sacrificed. If you keep silent now they will die. Your companions in the mountains will live regardless of what you say to me. You have the power of life and death over these people in the throng by the lake."

The stone mason relented and told Xlita "I was in the mountains with my kinsman and with a boy Treoc the arrow makers son. No others were with us. We hoped to escape the end of the world by hiding in cave, the way the heroes do in our old legends. My kinsman is still hidden but the boy ran away I know not where."

Now that he knew that the stonemason had fled with just two companions to a cavern in the mountains Xlita felt relieved. Most of the people had come back to the village as the water subsided and had been easily herded to the swollen lake. They were cowed by the priests, compliant in times of crisis and fearful of the gods.

The stonemason also feared the gods but he had the ability to act independently and at times contrarily. Xlita knew the man had been a less than willing labourer on the high priest's excavation and he sensed that the stonemason's fear of the gods was not combined with the usual penchant for evoking the gods to destroy their enemies or attempting to bribe them for long life or a fruitful harvest.

In fact, the stonemason felt that the gods probably could not be placated by humanity and that the only hope was to hide from their baleful gaze and avoid them if at all possible. Disturbing their places of rest or being in the presence of their images unsettled him. He felt the same way about the priesthood. He feared the priests greatly and did all he could to avoid contact with them.

To his great relief Xlita was true to his word and he did not summarily execute anyone from the crowd.

At this point, the high priest awoke from his reverie and stretched his hands out in the direction of the sun. "See how precarious his path through the sky has become!" called the high priest. Soon the sun will topple from heaven and rain fire upon the earth. This will be the last stage of the destruction of the world. Our one hope to avert the disaster lies in sacrifice to Tlaloc and Quetzalcoatl. This sacrifice is necessary to hold the sun on his course to avert the coming disaster."

The sunset looked like any other. Red light shone from the west and the fiery sunlight was reflected by the lake surface making it look like everything was aflame.

"A sacrificial victim must be chosen! I will ask the gods for guidance in choosing the offering. Quetzalcoatl will guide me to the right heart and then he will consume it. No one can tell what the appetite of the god will be or how much blood he will demand. I see a time when my acolytes will slaughter victims by the hundred and their hearts will support the weight of the sun in its fiery path across the heavens. This is the future if we are spared destruction. The appetite of the gods cannot easily be sated by mortals."

His new acolytes chose a man from the crowd. The man was tall and strong in comparison to their victims so far who had mostly been old and weak.

"His heart shall go to the feathered snake Quetzalcoatl!" cried the acolytes. The man struggled with the pair and wrested a knife from the man. He struck the man in the shoulder with it and made good his escape.

The high priest was furious. "This blasphemer presumes to escape and imperil us all. I feel the gods rage at being cheated of his heart. The sun shakes in the sky and our ruin comes closer than ever! Apprehend the man at all costs."

The rest of the acolytes who until now had taken no part in proceedings scrambled to pursue the escapee. The man had fled into the jungle that covered the hills to the north of the lake and the acolytes were stirred into hot pursuit.

The high priest composed himself somewhat and spoke "We need another victim."

The injured acolyte had staunched the flow of blood from the wound in his shoulder and he was attempting to recuperate. The woman selected a frail looking old man from the crowd and ushered him a knifepoint to the high priest.

The high priest slit the man's throat with ritual precision. Then he allowed the blood to spill into a bowl before cutting out the victim's heart. He held the heart up jubilantly to the crowd and chanted "Quetzalcoatl, Quetzalcoatl." He then threw the organ down onto the sand in front of the idol and let out a fierce yell.

The sun was setting. The day would soon be over and there was no sign of fire from the sky. The crowd were cold and hungry in the wet. Disoriented after the flood and confused by the high priest and the sudden emergence of the new acolytes and the idol.

Xlita had watched the struggle with interest. He felt that perhaps the crowd's mood was about to turn against the new acolytes and perhaps the people would even rebel against the high priest. This was just what he was waiting for to seize control. Xlita felt that it was vitally important that the priesthood retain control He was ready to order the acolytes to return from their futile hunt for the fugitives but the high priest still retained power.

Somehow he mesmerised the populace and not a few looked for the end of the world in the sky and trembled. Xlita thought that the high priest's power would wane when the sun set and the fire from the sky did not arrive. The coming night would also hinder his communication with the crowd and thus they would be left to their own devices to wonder about their survival and the fact that the world around them remains sodden but untouched by fire.

Xlita thought that sunrise would be his earliest opportunity to strike. When the sun made his journey undisturbed from the east into the heavens then the people would see that the gods are immutable and that although disasters blight the earth there is something permanent in the heavens to which humanity should pray and offer sacrifice to through the proper agency of their priesthood.

Outright rebellion was the least of Xlita's desires. When the people refused to obey the high priest, he would step in and assume control. A power vacuum was unthinkable and the acolytes he was sure would obey him.

To ensure that rebellion did not foment people that he found to be too independent in their behaviour had to be controlled. It was necessary to recapture the strong man who escaped today and Xlita bent his will to the task.

The high priest was absorbed in a reverie over blood and was entranced by the hearts before the idol.

"The god yearns for heart's blood and will not be sated by the paltry sacrifices we have made.", droned the high priest. "We must find those who have escaped and send them to the gods. The feathered snake writhes and snaps his jaws in anticipation of their blood. We must not disappoint him."

Some of the acolytes found the fugitive man in the jungle. They threw a poisoned spear at the man and hit their target. He was soon exhausted and they were able to overpower him and carry him back to the clearing near the lake.

The new acolytes were delighted and the wounded acolyte gloated over the victim. The high priest spoke "Fugitive you have angered the gods. Your proper place is as our messenger to Quetzalcoatl to plead for the lives of your fellows and to sustain or world by shedding your heart's blood. This is an honour you are accorded. Now die and go to Quetzalcoatl." And the high priest slit the man's throat and cut out his heart.

"These victims are blessed!" cried the high priest. "They go to Quetzalcoatl to dance before him and plead for the lives of we who remain. They will not live to be burnt to a cinder in great pain when the fire falls from the sky or to see their love ones consumed when the earth opens to swallow them up. The gods demand sacrifice!"

As the high priest spoke these words, the sun set and the folk were plunged into darkness. Xlita caused a fire to be lit and the high priest and the acolytes were visible to the people in its smoky light.

The high priest raised his arms heavenward and looked to the west where the sun had just set. "Soon our torment comes from the west, the sun has fallen from the sky and his flames will engulf the earth. Woe betide those who are burnt by the flames of the sun or are swallowed by the earthquakes of Tlaloc better to die now than in what is to come."

The clouds had parted in the course of the late afternoon and now stars shone down on the people.

The acolytes hunting for fugitives in the hills came back to the lakeshore, anticipating new orders from Xlita or the high priest himself. No orders were forthcoming. The high priest was in a reverie of sorrow and curious religious extasy and Xlita was occupied with the stonemason.

The people were hungry and in defiance of the high priest's certain wrath some of them took off for the village to take on some provender. Presently people came back to the lakeshore with what little meat and fruit they could salvage from the flood-ravaged village. Some others tried to catch fish in the swollen waters and the tense atmosphere at the lakeside where the people had been dismayed and confused dissipated somewhat.

The night sky was familiar and the stars shone brightly. The birds had returned after the storm and were warbling their dusk tunes. The end of the world seemed as far away now as a thousand centuries and the people took heart by doing familiar things.

Xlita noticed that the tension had gone out of the crowd. The distraction was welcome and he saw an opportunity to seize power. If he could keep the people feasting and gathering food then he could distract them from the high priest's prophecy of doom.

He bade the acolytes to fish in the lake and convinced Thalick (who had a very loud voice and was fond of oration) to tell a tale of the corn harvest. The people listened to the storyteller and forgot their woes. The acolytes caught many fish and a feast was prepared.

Xlita found acrobats amongst the crowd and had them entertain everyone with juggling and tumbling.

The high priest was at first oblivious to the people's fun. Guessing that they needed to eat to keep their strength up and feeling himself quite drained from his wound, he did not begrudge the folk their portion. He scanned the sky nervously, looking for signs of fire from heaven. He saw several meteors but nothing as spectacular as he had described the downfall of the sun to be.

He was sure that the sun had suffered a major calamity. The prophecies all spoke of this, the end of the sun and the end of the world. He took a morsel of fish from one of the acolytes and chewed it distractedly. This was the first food he had eaten in three days and he felt light headed and somewhat drowsy. This was how he often felt when a vision was about to come upon him.

The people were laughing at the capers of the acrobats and feeling reassured by the normalness of the proceedings. They certainly weren't thinking about the end of the world at this moment mused Xlita but they needed to show proper respect for the priesthood of course. Xlita knew he would have to cut their revel short. He was engaged in reflecting on how to grab and hold their attention when the high priest let out a moan and feinted. Xlita rushed to his side. The high priest had obviously been overcome by his wound and the strenuous nature of his exertions over the last three days. He checked the man's heartbeat and disappointedly concluded that the high priest was still alive. He bade the acolytes to place the high priest on his litter and there the unconscious potentate remained unmoving.

Xlita was encouraged by this turn of events." The high priest has gone on a heavenly journey to meet Quetzalcoatl", said Xlita, "Quetzalcoatl will recount to him the new way that the people are to live. He has decided to spare us all from destruction! Listen to the priests and all will be made clear."

He then gathered all of the acolytes to himself and said quietly and earnestly to them "Talk of the end of the world is divisive and deadly for our folk. We should talk to them of the harvest and the hunt and small things of the earth. The high priest drove us almost to destruction. I will make things different now. The people look to us for guidance we must be strong and in control and not enamoured of fantasies and wild talk of the end of the world. The feathered snakes breath blows still from the west and Tlaloc's rain has ceased. The gods do what they are bound to do and the pattern is repeated endlessly. In the natural order we are the interpreters of the gods' will and thus the leaders of the people. Accept my guidance and the priests will rule as a chosen race apart. The priesthood will be inherited from father to son at the will of the gods and there will be no upstart acolytes. No radical appointments that disturb nature."

The couple who had assisted the high priest with sacrifice were not privy to Xlita's instruction. They feasted with the others but the people were afraid of them and kept their distance. "We are heroes! We have averted Quetzalcoatl's wrath by timely sacrifice they cried. Give us our due we have saved you from a fate worse than death at the end of all things. Quetzalcoatl needs blood and we are the priest and priestess of his cult. We will see that the feathered snake supps on blood and partakes of a freshly beating heart as often as needs be. For this are we destined."

They took what bread and meat that they would and the people were too frightened to refuse it and they drank deep draughts and sang wild songs.

Xlita was disturbed by the new acolytes. Their appointment was against the natural order and they had committed excesses that no ordinary person should be allowed to commit. He did not know what to do with them. To simply execute them would be touted as ritual sacrifice and would set them up as demigods in a cult of bloodshed – something Xlita wanted very much to avoid. His preferred option was some form of exile or accident for the pair.

The stonemason was his other problem. He was tempted to release the man but did not like his superstitious fear of the priests and the gods. In a time of pious obedience such a man could scarcely do much harm but now that Xlita was going to manipulate the people's religious credulity and eliminate their fear of the immediate end of the world, he did not want anyone to cast doubt on the righteous domination of the priests and still less to suggest that they were people to avoid.

He wanted the people to be suspicious of the stonemason, to think that his fear of the priests was tantamount to unbelief and that he was an unlucky companion. Undoubtedly the people were afraid of the high priest but still bowed to his authority. Xlita wanted to maintain the priestly authority at all costs, even when it meant retaining the high priest and coping with the resulting excesses and slaughter. He had allowed the people a holiday to bring an orderliness to what threatened to become a rout and he was thankful that the high priest had passed out.

His greatest challenge was to convince the high priest himself that danger had passed and the gods had reconsidered their quest to destroy the world. How the high priest would react to the continued existence of the sun and the apparent indifference of the gods was a puzzle to Xlita. Would he press on with his blood fuelled sacrifices in a bid to hold the gods in appeasement or would he return to the traditions of his fathers (as Xlita hoped) and abandon the slaughter? Xlita knew he did not have much time to put his plans into action. The third possibility – that the high priest might not wake up cheered Xlita considerably. The high priest was wounded, poisoned and exhausted by hunger and exertion so it was possible that he might not recover. Xlita thought he had until morning. He had much to do.

The stone mason received something to eat from his captors and got some impression of the feasting and goings on that ensued. He could not move his arms or legs and had limited vision of the events beyond the circle of acolytes but he could tell that the mood had changed and that there was some activity afoot. He thought about his companions and wondered what his relative and the boy were doing.

Treoc and his companion were dry if not warm in their cave. They struggled to light a fire with wet kindling and had to be content with their lot. There was no sign of pursuit and none of the acolytes appeared to be anywhere near them in the jungle, which was fortunate. They knew only that they were sought after and that the stone mason had been captured. In this situation, seeking the village seemed unwise and they were content to wait in the cave for some change in the situation. They would be forced out for food eventually but the forest was vast and they hoped they might elude capture by the acolytes for a long time. The prophesised end of the world was nigh and Treoc was not certain that some cataclysm would not strike.

The man told the boy tales of the gods and heroes of the distant past and Treoc eventually fell asleep.

The people were well fed and weary. Xlita bade them to go home. This crazed vigil for the end of the world was to end and everyone was to return to the village.

After the flood the village offered comparatively little by way of shelter but the site was important and Xlita wanted a return to normality more than anything. They picked up the high priest and bore him back to the temple solemnly as befitted an injured leader and the last of the acolytes made their way to the temple, leaving the lake shore desolate and unwatched.

The two new acolytes returned to the temple. Their curious behaviour made them reluctant to return to their old homes and the temple although it might be a prison for them was also a sign of new status and security. The other acolytes gave them a wide berth. Xlita hesitated to give any instructions concerning them as he was frightened that the high priest might awake and demand their presence. He told his most trusted servants however that they were to be watched carefully and securely housed.

"We have served the gods well. Our reprieve seems certain as the world is not yet destroyed." said the man.

"More blood is needed to sustain the sun." replied the woman, "That was the high priest's task for us to keep the altars full with sacrifices and to spill glorious blood to appease Quetzalcoatl and dark Tlaloc. I feel the joyous rush of the god when I cut into the arteries of the victim. The beating heart transports its power to the sun as we look upon it and I feel the hunger of the feathered snake and the flood of triumph that flows through the rain god. These weak men, the other acolytes are not like the high priest. They lack his vision and would have our people go back to sleep when we have awoken to something glorious. I could never return to my old life now that I have become a servant of the gods. We must seek out the idol and worship it."

The idol had been brought back to the temple by several of the acolytes and it lay now in the great audience chamber undisturbed and unwatched. The idol made Xlita uneasy as did all new and unexpected things but he could think of no reason to leave it behind and it was senseless to instruct the people and the acolytes to ignore the enthrallingly lifelike figure of Quetzalcoatl.

The two new acolytes made their way to the audience chamber. They prostrated themselves in front of the statue of Quetzalcoatl and cried the god's name. The woman took a knife and pricked her finger and rubbed the blood into the idol.

"We must feed Quetzalcoatl with heart's blood and let him feast on human flesh." intoned the woman. She took the knife and traced a pattern on the man's arm with it. Small rivulets of blood flowed and she smeared the blood on the idol and on the man's forehead. They sang to the god and bowed low before the idol.

Xlita saw them worshipping the idol and he came up with a plan to be rid of the couple.

"This idol is indeed holy." Xlita said to them. "It deserves a special place apart reserved for it and those who serve it. I think it would be for the best if we return the idol whence it came. You can worship it in the hallowed cave where it was found and make a temple to Quetzalcoatl in this place. It is true that it is far from here but you will surely not let that daunt you. I will have acolytes assist you in transporting the idol to the cave and you will be able to worship Quetzalcoatl in a special place reserved for him alone. Priestess and priest of this new temple you can worship Quetzalcoatl in whatever way the gods instruct you."

"The god deserves no less." they responded. "We will accompany the idol and start a new temple to the god. The god demands sacrifice and we are the servants of Quetzalcoatl. Send us victims for sacrifice this is no less than the god's due already he hungers for heart's blood and grows impatient with his people."

Xlita called four of his most trusted acolytes without delay. They were instructed to bear the statue back to the cave from whence it came and to see that the new acolytes arrived safely at the location of the new temple.

Xlita intended to exile the new acolytes to the cave and leave them to be forgotten. The cave was far away from the village and most of the populace were unaware of its existence and location. The idol too would be gone and hopefully the alarming new rites would fade from the people's memory. Xlita promised to send sacrifices to the new temple – a promise he had no intention of keeping and bade the new acolytes and the idol bearers to be on their way.

They left the temple and made the long journey to the cave without incident. The going was hard for the idol bearers only one of whom knew the way. The new acolytes were disoriented as Xlita had told the man to be deliberately vague about the path. They were in high spirits however as they had gotten the recognition they believed the deserved. A place apart to worship the god with no constraints or meddling from the other priests.

The acolytes charged with handling the idol hurriedly took their leave of the new acolytes and they were left alone in the cave with the idol.

Xlita's strategy would prove only partially effective. Whilst the new acolytes were never to return to the village or the temple. They were not completely forgotten and strange disappearances took place from the village. Dead beasts were often found near the cave. Putative offerings to those that served the god and of the disappearances it was said that they perished on the altar of the new temple.

The new acolytes became the forerunners of a new tribe with other bloodier customs and gods hungry for the beating human heart. Indeed, they would outlast the people from the village and the temple and the gods would be remembered as being thirsty for human blood.

Xlita merely knew that he had solved a thorny problem. His greatest remaining problem slept soundly. The high priest had fallen into a deep sleep and was feverish, which was not surprising in view of his wounds and the extent to which he had exerted himself over the last few days.

Xlita also retired to bed, feeling secure in his role as the true power broker.

The next morning, Treoc and his companion awoke. They woke up with the passing of time, oblivious to whether it was light or dark outside the cave. They decided to chance a look speculating about the possible end of the world and the rain of fiery oblivion that was to strike the outside world. They went to the cave mouth and were greeted by glorious sunshine. No clouds were to be seen in the sky and the sun looked secure on his path through the heavens. This cheered them greatly and they decided to risk finding some food. They collected berries and mushrooms and tried to spear fish in the creek.

"The end of the world has been averted." said the man. "The high priest is wrong. The world has not come to an end. Many still fear him though and I do not think it is safe for us to return to the village (if anything is left of it after the flood)."

They spent the day outside grateful for the good weather and freedom from the draughty cave.

The high priest awoke groggy and confused at first. He did not know how he came to be in the temple on his litter and he was aware that he had something very urgent to do. That the end of the world was irrevocably nigh. He stumbled to a window and looked out. The sun rode high in a clear, cloudless blue sky. What was he to make of this? He had thought that the sun was cast down from his path through the heavens and that fire and chaos were the lot of the earth.

Could there be a problem with the prophecy? Had he miscalculated – perhaps it would take another day for Tlaloc to shake the sun free of his heavenly course. That must be it. The sun was a powerful god in himself an assault from the rest of the heavenly host would not lead to immediate downfall. They were just experiencing the calm before the storm.

Still it disturbed the high priest that he had misinterpreted the omens. Destruction of the world was clearly foretold but perhaps he was wrong about the timeframe. Three days was a short time. He would reread the knots on the tapestry. He made to rise only to find that his leg gave him searing pain. Wounded and disoriented as he was he was also no longer sure that three days had past. Perhaps this was the morning of the third day and in his dizzy fevered state he had imagined the sun setting one more time than it had?

Confused as he was he needed to clear his head and come to a decision about how best to face the ensuing end of the world. He called out "acolytes, servants of the temple come to me!"

A young acolyte hurriedly made his way into the chamber where the high priest lay on his litter.

"What is your bidding master?" the acolyte asked.

"How many days have past since the eclipse of the sun?"

"Today is the fourth day my lord." replied the acolyte.

"Assemble the people we must make sacrifices at the lakeshore." commanded the high priest.

"Holy one I must ask lord Xlita. You have been unwell and Xlita makes the decisions for us. He said that you were consumed by your visions of the feathered snake and that we must look to him for guidance. I am sure he will concur with you."

The high priest was enraged "I am the high priest of the temple. If Xlita doubts this I will cut out his heart and offer it to the gods."

The acolyte fled in terror.

The high priest grasped for support, found a stick and rose painfully to his feet. He staggered off the raised platform that contained the litter and strode purposefully out the door and into the corridor that lead to the tapestry. He would see if the knots read the same as he remembered.

He came to the tassellated tapestry and examined the knots at its base. The knots spoke of a blackening of the sun, a flood and then fire and extermination and the great wrath of Quetzalcoatl and Tlaloc, the destroyers of the world. Three suns were to pass. Three suns meant undoubtedly three days. The knots held no comfort for the high priest.

Perhaps thought the high priest, the war in heaven goes the sun's way for a while and the other gods cannot lightly unseat him. The struggle could take some time. New sacrifices were required and he needed the god's guidance it would be good to feel the wind and to see the idol and think on Quetzalcoatl. First however he had to deal with Xlita's insubordination. The man was insufferably arrogant. The high priest knew that Xlita was a noble who disapproved of the new acolytes and held that the priesthood should be inherited.

In this the high priest felt he was moved by the whim of the gods and the frenzied behaviour of his new acolytes suggested divine possession. The extreme circumstances also called for new customs and above all for religious rites and sacrifices. The gods were angered and wide awake as the populace would find out at their peril. He would have the people assemble at the lakeside before the idol and he would select a sacrifice and be overcome by the god who would doubtless explain to him what he had to do and how the prophecy should be properly interpreted.

The high priest hobbled to Xlita's chamber. He knocked on the door, waking the man within. Xlita called out angrily "Who dares disturb my slumber."

"It is me.", replied the high priest.

"Holy one. I beg your forgiveness I had reckoned with one of the lesser acolytes. Come in."

"Why was I brought back to the temple? My instructions were clear. We were all to wait by the lakeside for the final stages of the end of the world."

"You lost consciousness my lord and I thought it best that you were brought to a safe place to recover. The people were exhausted and I had to send them home."

"War is waged in heaven. The gods seek to overthrow the sun. The struggle has gone on longer than three days and the gods are no doubt angry and frustrated. We must sacrifice to them to mitigate."

"The prophecy could as well mean three centuries hence as three days. Or a day when three suns are in the sky. The texts are confusing and there is doubt…"

"I have no doubt that the end of the world is nigh, Xlita. Make ready to depart for the lakeside!"

"As you will holy one, it shall be done."

Xlita was not ready to move openly against the high priest. The high priest was revered and feared by almost everyone. The failure of the world to end might damage the reverence with which he was held but the people still feared him as a bringer of death and destruction. They would go back to the lakeshore. Xlita instructed the acolytes to round up the populace and bring them to the shores of the lake once more.

The high priest was incensed to find that his two chosen acolytes were gone. "They have gone to the new temple.", said an acolyte. This angered the high priest considerably. Xlita had shown signs of arrogance and insubordination he could not tolerate. The high priest beat the messenger with his stick in irritation at the message he had brought.

Limping painfully, the high priest made his way to the great audience chamber and his litter. Some acolytes lifted the litter and carried the high priest out of the temple and to the lake shore.

Once they were at the lake shore, the high priest stood up and looked around. The people were gathered in a confused mass at the lakeside. The acolytes were there in force, herding them closer to the shore. The idol was gone, much to the high priest's distress, another liberty on Xlita's part he thought. Soon Xlita would not be making light of the high priest's plans anymore. The high priest would send him to the gods to explain himself!

The acolytes and the people were now assembled on the lakeside. Xlita was in the middle of a group of acolytes some distance from the high priest.

The high priest was at a part of the lake where the ground fell away steeply and the water was very deep. "The gods demand sacrifice!" cried the high priest. "The war in heaven goes toward the ultimate destruction of the sun. We have only achieved a brief hiatus the rain of fire from the sky will certainly come."

"I will take Xlita as my sacrifice. Bring him to me!" commanded the high priest of a burly acolyte that stood nearby.

"Lord I cannot. He is the heir to the high priesthood and I am but a humble acolyte."

The enraged high priest lunged at the acolyte with his dagger. The man stepped aside, alarmed, and the high priest overbalanced and fell into the deep water. He struggled for a while and then went under, dragged down as if by some invisible water monster.

The crowd watched stunned by the high priest's sudden disappearance.

Xlita addressed them. "The high priest has gone to the gods blessed be his name! The gods will not end the world today or tomorrow. I think. The prophecy is ambiguous and thus I believe it will be centuries before our world ends. As the new high priest, I bid you all go home!"

The people went home. The human sacrifices came to an end in the village and Xlita reigned as high priest. Xlita freed the stone mason who went into the hills in search of Treoc and his relative. When he found them, he told them of the high priest's death and they returned to the village.

Treoc lived to be an old man and saw the sun get swallowed by the moon a second time. This time there was no flood and the village priests said it was an ill omen but they did nothing except smoke and dance to Quetzalcoatl. He wondered sometimes what the fire in the sky would be like when the sun finally toppled from the sky. One day the world would end but the new priests said it would not be in their lifetimes.

Milton Keynes UK
Ingram Content Group UK Ltd.
UKHW010610291123
433416UK00001B/260